About the author

Anne was born and raised in Northern Idaho near Pend Oreille Lake in the small rural town of Sandpoint. Writing was always a passion. But it wasn't until her late 50s when she was able to fulfil her dream and write her first novel. 'All In a Daydream' which came out in 2020. Thanks to Pegasus Publishing, who also printed her second book 'Dreams Come True?' in 2021. The trilogy will now be complete with her third book, 'The Dreamer'. What started out as a way to deal with the loss of a best friend, ended up creating an author.

THE DREAMER

Anne Nelson

THE DREAMER

Vanguard Press

VANGUARD PAPERBACK

© Copyright 2024
Anne Nelson

The right of Anne Nelson to be identified as author of
this work has been asserted by her in accordance with the
Copyright, Designs and Patents Act 1988.

All Rights Reserved

No reproduction, copy or transmission of this publication
may be made without written permission.
No paragraph of this publication may be reproduced,
copied or transmitted save with the written permission of the
publisher, or in accordance with the provisions
of the Copyright Act 1956 (as amended).

Any person who commits any unauthorised act in relation to this
publication may be liable to criminal prosecution and civil claims
for damages.

A CIP catalogue record for this title is available from the British
Library.

ISBN 978-1-80016-943-2

This is a work of fiction. Names, characters, businesses, places, events and
incidents are either the products of the author's imagination or used in a
fictitious manner. Any resemblance to actual persons, living or dead, or
actual events is purely coincidental.

Vanguard Press is an imprint of
Pegasus Elliot Mackenzie Publishers Ltd.
www.pegasuspublishers.com

First Published in 2024

Vanguard Press
Sheraton House Castle Park
Cambridge England

Printed & Bound in Great Britain

Dedication

To Lee. My forever.

Acknowledgements

Thank you to all the authors who have delighted, educated, amused and entertained me throughout my life. And to all the support from my friends and family.

MONDAY

Becca woke with a start.

She was beyond thrilled to find herself in their stateroom with Cain's arms securely wrapped about her.

Her relief was undeniable.

Yet the feeling of loss was still on her mind.

What a weird fucking dream.

As she told Cain, it took place at the cabin and she thought *she recalled her brother James being there and her youngest nephew Jake.*

But the more she tried to remember, the fuzzier it all became. The thought of her brother made her a bit sad;since they had a falling out a few years back and she really missed her youngest nephew, they'd always been close with a very special bond. They still talked but not like they used to, not since she stopped talking to her brother.

As dreams go, it wasn't exactly bad, not until the end when she stood at an airport or it could have been a dock at a marina, all she knew for certain is that she was waiting for Cain and feeling the heart crushing pain of losing him forever when he didn't arrive. Very odd how the mind works.

Still, at that moment of sheer panic; it became the most real and worst nightmare she'd ever had. The pain seemed so real. Almost unbearable and just thinking about it brought tears to her eyes.

Maybe, it was a good thing that the particulars were becoming just a fog, deep in her psyche.

Nonetheless, her heart had a small ache from the only thing she recalled with certainty, missing him. Frantically and painfully missing him!

'Thank God Cain woke me up!' She sighed with true relief.

Now, as she looked over at her handsome man, she couldn't help but smile, she loved him so very much. Her heart told her she was where she was meant to be.

And having him right beside her, the feeling of loss began to diminish into oblivion.

Cain seemed to always sense when she was awake and watching him. He moved his hand down her back to her lovely bare ass and gave her a squeeze.

His touch consistently stirred her desire.

"Morning baby. You feeling better now?"

Oh, how she relished his touch.

"Yes, my love, very." It was a tad breathy; since he was arousing the hell out of her with his gentle caresses.

"You know Becca, it's been well over a week since you wore one of your dresses." He winked and smiled before claiming her lips as his own.

In his love she forgot about the bizarre dream and resumed her fantasy with the ever amorous and skilfully adept, Mr. Curtis.

After their shower that morning, she did wear the shorter of the two dresses with bra and panties.

No need scaring the staff before breakfast.

She had noticed a small red welt on her ass when she looked in the mirror and asked Cain if he'd pinched her.

He nodded.

"Yep. Sometime in the middle of the night you informed me; I wasn't real so, I pinched you. I actually didn't realise until after that, that you were sound asleep, but once I pinched you, you settled right back into my arms and seemed more at peace." He kissed her cheek and escorted her to the galley.

As they were drinking their first cup of coffee, Cain let her know that he had to make a few conference calls that morning.

Once they were done eating, and before he headed into his study, he reminded her he would be wanting full access just after lunch.

With a wink, a very nice kiss, he left, leaving Becca with some major anticipation as he disappeared behind closed doors.

Yep, she was quite flush. Again.

'Damn that man!'

She needed a distraction. Even after their ardent morning, she was feeling 'frustrated' for lack of going into more details, which really shouldn't be necessary… don't you agree?

'What the hell has that man done to me?'

She went from no sex for well over a decade, to missing it after just two short hours.

She couldn't' help but smile.

He was a force.

Joel gave her a curious look. She gave him a wink and went to change her clothes.

Since they were still docked in the Port of Seattle and weren't scheduled to leave until the late afternoon tide, she'd have time to go for a nice long walk.

The plan was made the day before, that the Kid, aka Kevin, would drive Frank's SUV down to San Diego to meet back up with 'SIRA'; when she arrived five days after her departure from Puget Sound.

At just over thirteen hundred nautical miles, and the yachts top speed of eighteen knots, it was the best educated guess the captain could give his young son.

But of course, he would not be caravanning alone, Joel's boyfriend Steve would be driving Becca's Enclave since she was staying on the yacht with Cain.

No need to rehash that argument. 'YIKES!'

Cain was at least good enough to ask if it would be okay; he didn't assume, and that made her happy.

Truth be told... she was quite content staying with her man and not having to deal with stupid drivers over three states.

Just a tad bit of road rage when it came to others ineptness behind the wheel... that and she liked to push the parameters of posted speed limits... by quite a bit.

Everyone has a vice... don't judge.

Steve worked as a freelance reporter, and when Cain asked him if he'd be interested in driving the second vehicle, he jumped at the opportunity. He had missed Joel quite a bit and this would give him a chance to spend a little more time with his boyfriend, at least on the drive home.

When Becca found out the name of Joel's significant, she instantly thought of another quote from her favorite movie, 'all gay men are named Mark, Rick or Steve.'

She didn't even have to say a word... Joel knew exactly where her thoughts were and grinned. It turned out to be one of his favorite movies as well.

Not a huge shocker... Becca called him 'girlfriend' for the rest of that day.

She already adored Joel and now that he loved 'Steel Magnolia's' too, she now thought of him as one of her favorite people.

And a dear friend.

Cain had made the decision to stay the extra time in Seattle to get 'SIRA' ready for the warmer waters of California, as well as give Joel and Steve a night together on the town; as well as the entire crew. They had earned a well-deserved break for a night or two. This of course included he and Becca.

A very popular decision since everyone on the boat enjoyed getting back on land for a few hours.

Even the Captain and Mrs Abbot took a nice break to have a date night, just the two of them.

Cain and Becca revisited Aqua and enjoyed another wonderful evening and this time she was fully awake for the entire meal. *And yes, she still disliked oysters.*

On this, their last day in port and while Cain was busy working, Becca decided to wander around the harbor again.

The first time, you may remember, was before they even left for Alaska, when shit hit the fan because she bought dinner for the crew.

Now of course, that event seemed petty and amusing to everyone, but poor Joel.

Freshly changed into jeans and a light sweater, since there always seemed to be a cool breeze coming off the Sound, and that short dress was not the right attire for wind or her walk. Becca headed down the two flights of stairs to the very back deck.

While she was enjoying her stroll, she called Mary.

It had been too long; since she and her friend had a chance to catch up… and after the interesting week she'd had on their trip south from Alaska; she really wanted to hear her best friend's voice.

Mary had, of course, responded to Becca after she'd sent that photo bomb email showing her the glacier, the bears, the raptor center, the Tram and of course Cain...that was the email where she gave her bestie two thumbs up with a 'wholly shit is he hot'.

Becca loved Mary and her honest opinion.

She herself had the same thoughts regarding her man.

"You're what? What do you mean you're not coming back right away? Okay... don't get me wrong, he's a looker but Becs, you do or did have a life here as well. And besides that, I was hoping for a three or four-hour hug; since I'm missing the crap out of you. And in saying all that, I know you deserve to be happy and having regular sex so I'll begrudgingly accept the fact that I don't get to see you for another week or so... but that's it. Do you hear me?"

She was on a roll, and Becca knew better than to even try to butt in.

Finally, a pause to breath. 'Yes, small favors'.

"Of course, I'll be back... and we'll have loads of time to catch up. I promise you. And besides, you know it was never my intention to leave for this long. But seriously Mary it's been so wonderful and amazing. A true 'once in a lifetime' experience and, I've fallen in love with him. I mean I really truly love him. I've never felt this way about anyone, ever. And here's a huge shocker, I am pretty sure he loves me too." She hoped her friend could feel her unmistakable joy over the phone.

She could and did and finally told Becca that she deserved to be loved and always had and then told her to travel safe and; she looked forward to seeing her sooner rather than later and meeting her new 'hubba hubba' in person.

Just talking to her friend made her fantasy seem all the more real.

She was all smiles, when she headed back to the yacht.

Unfortunately, she was the only one.

Cain looked like he swallowed a lemon when she got back on board.

"Hey babe, did you have a nice walk?" His smile didn't reach his eyes.

Without missing a beat, she wrapped her arms around him.

He sighed and held her tight. She knew something wasn't right in his world.

"Cain, what's wrong? Is there anything I can do to help?" She could count on one hand how many times that he had showed any sign of distress or unhappiness. Okay, maybe two but still, not a lot.

Without answering her question directly, he hugged her even tighter and asked if she'd please go put her dress back on. He was in need of a pleasant diversion if she were agreeable.

No need to press him since he wasn't ready to talk. Instead, she nodded into his chest and knew that her response put a huge grin on his face.

As she headed to their stateroom, he patted her ass and reminded her no underwear.

Oh yeah... huge blush.

Well... that turned out to be one amazing afternoon of distractions for them both. It started in her closet, as she was undressing and ended in the entertainment room where they had gone to watch a movie and take a much-needed breather... well that was the original plan.

DAMN!

Becca was sound asleep in the recliner when the captain announced that they would be departing in half an hour, and his booming voice over the loudspeaker woke her up and she realised that she was stiff and quite sore.

She giggled at the thought of being 'road hard and put up wet'.

As she looked around the dark room, she realised that Cain wasn't there but had covered her with a blanket before he left. Very considerate and much appreciated; since she didn't have a stitch of clothing on and needed to find her dress before she could leave the theatre room.

She had just wrapped the blanket around her; when the door opened and the lights went on.

Deer in the headlights comes to mind.

"Sorry baby. I thought you'd still be asleep."

He hit the dimmer switch.

She had to blink a few times to get the spots to leave her field of vision but finally noticed Cain was carrying a tray with two smoothies… Joel must have known they needed nutrients; since neither of them ate lunch.

Busy! Understatement to be sure.

That chef of his was smart and very attentive.

The thought made her smile.

When she first came on board, she was embarrassed around the crew but now she just took it in stride.

"Have you seen where my dress has disappeared to?" And took the smoothie he offered.

He nodded and gave her a wicked look.

"Drink up please."

And without another word pulled her onto his lap as he sat back in the recliner; she had just relinquished.

She took a sip. Joel outdid himself this time, it was pineapple, mango with a hint of coconut, YUM.

Cain's must have been delicious as well; since they both finished them in record time.

Sex can work up an appetite, that's for sure.

He set his glass on the floor and took hers to do the same, right about the time the engines kicked on.

"Did you want to go watch the captain take us out of port?"

He shook his head and reached under the blanket to caress her breasts.

Her whole body shivered and came alive with just that one intimate touch.

'Seriously, what the fuck have you done to me', was her first thought.

Her second was that she was still tired and as mentioned earlier, sore from their previous activities. But here she was again craving him, with every fiber of her being.

Really!

"Baby, are you too sore?" His lips were playing with her ear.

He always seemed to know what she'd been thinking.

She grinned and nodded before taking his lips to hers.

She hoped he locked the door.

After his fingers moved away from her breasts on a more southern trajectory... she couldn't' give a crap if the door was locked or not.

Cain was stroking her back after another very satisfying diversion, and they both jumped when there was a rather loud unexpected knock.

She couldn't' help but laugh.

Joel told them dinner would be ready in less than an hour, and that he was feeding everyone from the back deck.

Then there was silence.

She looked up into those amazing green eyes that she loved so dearly and told him; she was in fact quite hungry.

"Thank God, me too babe... I'm starving." He kissed her forehead.

He wrapped the blanket around her and told her to wait there and he'd be back in five. He pulled on his jeans and took their glasses and the tray as he headed out the door.

Damn that man looked good in just jeans... great ass. She made herself blush with that thought.

When he returned, he had her robe. Cain then escorted her to the guest room with the ensuite where she found a pair of jeans, a sweater, socks and shoes laid out on the bed. He stripped out of his pants and removed her robe before they both enjoyed a nice hot shower.

She was still a tad inquisitive wondering what happened to her dress.

But he wasn't giving that information away.

Once freshly showered Becca put on the jeans and sweater without bra or panties, shaking her head, and took his extended hand once, she had tied the laces up on her shoes.

He led them out to the back deck to have dinner with the crew.

Joel barbequed salmon steaks with lemon butter, grilled asparagus and prepared a wonderful garden salad for everyone. And being the wonderful chef that he was, even surprised Becca with a delectable piece of grilled halibut.

She gave him a huge hug. And thanked him for the delicious smoothie and for providing her an alternative to salmon.

He actually blushed.

Such a girl.

Mrs Abbot got her plate and one for her husband and excused herself to go and eat with him on the bridge.

They were such a cute couple. Married just over twenty-seven years. Becca liked them very much.

During dinner, Frank and Cain got into a huge discussion regarding upgrades to the engine they could do once back in San Diego. Improvements that would help with fuel efficiency and make 'SIRA' more eco-friendly. A tad technical, and although Becca did try, she found it exceedingly boring.

She and Joel started their own discussion about the best lines from 'Steel Magnolia's' one of their favorite films, as mentioned earlier. He had memorized more lines than she had. 'So, gay!'

But they both agreed one of the best lines was 'I love you more than my luggage.' Their laughter made both Cain and Frank look over in a confused way... they each shook their head and went back to tech-talk.

That reaction caused Becca and Joel to laugh even harder.

She adored him more and more.

Plus, he was never offended by her sense of humor and sarcastic comments, he knew she respected him and his life choice.

And besides... Joel had a very evil sense of humor himself and could give as good as he could take. She considered him a very special friend.

Becca fell asleep sometime during that evening's festivities.

"Come on baby, let's get you to bed." Cain was chuckling as he picked her up.

"Just sleep, right?" She laid her head on his shoulder.

"Yes Becca. Just sleep." He kissed her forehead.

She ignored both Frank and Joel's laughter.

Once in their room she managed to change into a nightgown and brush her teeth on autopilot before climbing into bed.

She drifted back to sleep instantly and barely felt his arms wrap around her.

TUESDAY

The next morning, Becca woke alone in bed, but Cain left her a note letting her know he loved her and thanked her for being the best distraction he'd ever had and would see her at breakfast.

As usual, she kissed the note and went to put it in her closet; where she kept all his previous ones.

She was getting quite a nice collection, and she had an idea forming about what she would do with them... a memento perhaps.

Once showered and dressed she headed to the galley for a much-needed cup of coffee.

She had to make an effort to walk as normal as she could since their day of loving left her very sore. She'd not felt that sore since their first day having sex. Of course, both encounters had felt amazing and brought a smile to her face. It also made her realise that she and her vagina really missed her nice cool lake.

Light bulb!

'We're back in the lower forty-eight, perhaps I could take a dip in the ocean when we stop for fuel.'

One of her better ideas and a very pleasant one to boot.

Now the big question... when do they need to stop?

She really didn't know a lot about the inner workings of the yacht.

Joel wished her a 'good morning' as he handed her a cup of coffee and; she quizzed him about the boats fuel and schedule.

He shook his head and told her that he had no clue but thought they would top off the tank in Coos Bay, Oregon sometime the next day or day after if they didn't make any other detours.

He was a good eavesdropper and wonderful informant.

Joel was just handing her a second cup of coffee when Cain joined them.

She got all her answers from him.

'SIRA' can hold fifteen thousand gallons of fuel on board when full, but they usually kept her around ten thousand gallons and that's the reason they stopped more frequently.

'Jeez, that's like fifty thousand dollars if they did fill her up'. WOW! That blew Becca's mind.

Cain's sleek baby had the ability to go twenty-eight knots if he would allow Frank to take away some ballast, but he was fine with her only going eighteen knots. Made for a more enjoyable ride in his opinion, and he liked all his add-ons which made her a bit heavier than other yachts.

They would indeed top off in Coos Bay and again in Oakland before reaching their final destination, Kona

Kai Marina in San Diego. The whole trip would burn just over thirty-two thousand gallons of fuel.

'FUCK!' Again, that blew her mind.

Cain raised his eyebrow letting her know he knew she dropped the 'f' bomb in her head.

'Freak'.

He continued her education as Joel served them breakfast.

She was pleased when he handed her a fruit and yogurt parfait with some of his homemade granola, something light for a change. Cain's eyes lit up when Joel gave him biscuits and gravy.

And yes, she ate every bite. So, did Cain.

Since her stunningly handsome man was in a chatty mood, she asked about going swimming in the ocean when they docked for fuel.

"No, it will be too early in the morning for that, but I think we can do one better, and take a side trip into Tillamook Bay for your dip and then we can go pick up some amazing cheese and ice cream in the process." He had a huge grin just thinking about that.

Finally, he was back on topic. "Hold that idea and let me go check with the captain before I make you any promises I can't keep." He gave her a very nice kiss and thanked Joel for breakfast.

More talking to herself, "How that man does not weigh three hundred pounds is mind boggling." She was shaking her head and Joel busted out laughing.

Becca gave him a sideways glance, and he told her a little secret. "Miss Becca have you ever noticed that when Mr. Cain eats a heavy breakfast, he doesn't eat lunch or has a salad and dinner is protein and veggies only? Plus, he works out several mornings a week." He smiled at her as he started cleaning the galley.

Why hadn't she ever paid attention to that. 'For fuck's sake Becs, he watches your food intake like a hawk'. She'd do better in the future.

With that inner monologue finished, she went to put on her own workout clothes, and hit the treadmill to try and walk some of her soreness out and burn a few calories in the process.

Good in theory.

Here's a little titbit of information that skinny people don't understand. People who have weight issues have a problem of never seeing themselves thinner in mirrors. Pictures sometime help. But their body image may always plague them. And often does their entire lives.

Becca managed to walk for a good thirty minutes feeling a bit of a burn in the legs at the incline and pace. she put the machine at but still wanted an icepack to soothe her other ache.

Cain was in the doorway watching and scared the crap out of her when he spoke.

She almost fell on the treadmill but caught herself. She cursed at him under her breath.

"Sorry baby... are you okay? But seriously; didn't we have enough of a workout yesterday?" He chuckled.

She glared.

"I'll have you know; you broke my vagina."

And with that, went to walk by him.

He wasn't about to let that happen and pulled her into one of his bear hugs.

"I really am sorry I startled you. As for the other issue. Not sorry, not one little bit. But maybe your vagina just needs more use." She shook her head and saw that evil smile he gets when he's feeling frisky.

He gave her a rather passionate kiss that reminded her why she was so sore in the first place.

Damn him!

She pulled away from the kiss and put her head on his shoulder. She loved his hugs, and nothing made her feel more loved than his arms wrapped around her.

"What did the captain say?" Change in subject was needed.

He started to rub her back.

And her body started to respond to his touch.

Really! 'Fucking Traitor!'

"You're good to go with a swim in roughly three hours. Although Garibaldi Harbor isn't equipped with a dock big enough to accommodate 'SIRA' we'll have to anchor out in the bay and use the launch. But I found out where Steve and the 'Kid' are, they'll meet us at the marina, so we have a ride. The Creamery is only nine miles from where we'll dock, and I even found you a great little swimming hole called 'Kilchis Logging Bridge'. It's also about nine miles from the harbor so, we'll take you there first for your swim, and then we'll all go get some ice cream and cheese." He was wearing her favorite smile.

She thought that was a good idea, but she wanted to throw out one she felt was better.

"Why don't I go to the swimming hole with anyone else who wants to swim and you, Frank and Joel go to the Tillamook Creamery? After I'm done, I can come meet you there or we'll meet back at the dock."

Perfect compromise since she didn't need any cheese or ice cream, and she also knew that Joel wasn't a huge fan of swimming and Frank wasn't either, so why waste their time.

If you haven't been paying attention... Cain sucks at compromise.

His response wasn't at all surprising. "No. I'll take you. Now let's see about getting you out of those workout clothes and into a nice hot shower."

His lips were playing with her ear which was usually a huge turn on.

But she was getting miffed at his dismissive response.

She tried to pull out of his arms, but he wouldn't let her go.

"Becca, you know I'm not going to let you swim without supervision so please give me this. I can't enjoy being anywhere you're not."

He resumed kissing her neck.

She knew she'd give in, how could she not after that very sincere and honest statement.

Cain was back to her earlobe with those amazing lips.

She moaned and he knew he had her.

Did any of you doubt that for a minute. Oh, please.

They made it to the guest bedroom with the ensuite so they could shower before spending an hour or so in bed.

He managed to help her forget her soreness and relish in their intimate affection for one another.

He is a force.

And again, she wanted to know where the hell his stamina came from.

"Cain, you never told me what you needed a diversion from yesterday. I would like to help if I can." She was enjoying their closeness but knew something was still plaguing his thoughts.

"You're doing it, just by being here. I'm not ready to talk about that right now. You'll be the first to know when I am, okay?" He was caressing her bare ass and all of sudden gave it a very audible swat.

'Fuck that's hot' and her want for this man was up and running. With four more just like the first she lost all her composure and became quite primal in attacking her assailant.

His moans were louder than hers that time, and she was pleased to have the opportunity to use her newfound skill that put her in charge of his climax.

Becca woke before Cain. A rarity to be sure. And for once he didn't stir.

That gave her an idea.

NOPE! Minds out the gutter people she'd already been there done that.

It's not all about sex.

Yep, that made me laugh too.

She decided to leave him a note, like he did for her on so many occasions.

This was yet another occurrence that happened so rarely, she needed to take advantage.

After a short search in the bedside table, Becca put pen to paper.

My darling Cain,

I love being your distraction. And I am so blessed that you stopped for coffee six short weeks ago. You're my dream come true, and I love you with all my heart and soul. Forever yours, Becca.

She put her note on the pillow next to him and headed down to the main salon after putting on her workout clothes... a little smelly but it was all she had.

And before you ask, yes, she wanted another shower and sore doesn't even come close to describing her discomfort.

She winced taking the stairs. 'FUCK! I need an out of order sign... maybe 'closed for renovations' she laughed at that thought.

Becca was amazed, flabbergasted and surprised that she actually got through her whole shower alone and was even fully dressed before Cain joined her in their stateroom.

He was wearing her favorite smile and pulled her into his arms the minute he saw her.

"Baby, your note was the best thing I've ever read. And you are a dream come true for me as well." He gave her a very loving kiss before heading to take his own shower. If you have ever wondered what 'Cloud-Nine' would be like.

Becca reached it in the arms of her man that day.

When she made it back out to the salon to get some water, she realized they weren't moving, and Joel grinned telling her that everyone was going on an outing.

She knew his smile was more about seeing Steve than getting cheese, but it was nice all the same to see him so happy.

He and Steve had been together for just under four years, and this was the first time they'd spent this much time apart. It seemed to make them realize how much they really loved each other. They were a very adorable couple.

Becca was just finishing her bottle of water when Cain's arms came around her and he kissed her head.

"Ready to go baby?"

She was... she made sure to wear her suit under her shorts and shirt, and she put a pair of panties and bra in her bag for after her dip. And for the first time had her own cash. Not that he'd let her spend it... still she felt glad all the same for just having it.

Now, all she needed to do was grab a towel from the cabinet down by the launch.

He told her to grab two.

No huge surprise that Mrs. Abbot didn't want to go for their cheesy adventure and opted to get a bit of cleaning done while the boat was empty of its other residents. The captain also chose to stay on board since he wanted to get in a nap before the next leg of their journey. Neither seemed to get a lot of down time, in Becca's opinion, so she could see taking a few hours to just relax must seem wonderful to them both.

Cain did ask if they'd like for him to send their son out for a visit, but they both said that wasn't necessary since they just saw him two days prior.

Good parents, I mean what young man doesn't want to go and eat copious amounts of cheese and ice cream. Especially when the boss is buying.

So, Joel, Frank, Becca and Cain took the launch into the marina where they met their rides.

Steve and the 'Kid' apparently had to backtrack by just under eighty miles after getting Cain's call.

Nice guys, although technically, he is their employer. At least to the 'Kid'. And of course, Steve got to spend time with Joel. Win-win.

Cain took Becca's keys as they were the only ones going to the swimming hole.

The other four gentlemen were heading for the Tillamook Country Smoker and would meet up with the rest of their party at the Creamery a bit later in the day.

'Kilchis Logging Bridge' was true to its name. Just a nice swimming hole on the Kichis River. It was definitely an old logging road, and Becca was hoping her suspension would survive the drive, which was just a tad under a mile and a half from the highway.

Cain was being careful, but the road had certainly seen its share of traffic over the years and bumpy doesn't come close to describing its overall condition. The rough ride didn't help her other condition either. Yep, sore to the nth degree.

Once they arrived, Becca saw several campsites and of course lots of kids as well as adults were swimming, but nothing was going to stop her from taking her turn in the nice cool water.

The river made her think of a few, she grew up around in Northern Idaho. Many of those same rivers fed into her lake.

You know, the ones that you throw an inner tube on and float down with friends on a lazy summer's day.

Nice memory to be sure.

Becca instantly loved Cain's choice of where to take her swimming.

She was however, surprised to see that Cain had his suit on under his shorts and joined her for part of her swim.

The water was a tad chilly; which was perfect for Becca. He got out after ten minutes, telling her to swim as long as she'd like. He sat on the shore and watched.

She loved him more each and every day. If that's even possible.

Just over a half hour later; she emerged from the river where Cain wrapped her in a towel and his arms. She gave him a nice kiss and thanked him again for the wonderful treat.

"Baby, you don't need to thank me. The look on your face is worth any trip down a logging road." He faked a horrified expression that made her laugh.

They sat by the river for another twenty minutes giving Becca time to dry off a little and warm up in the afternoon sun. He never took his arms from around her.

She felt cherished by this incredible man.

It's the little things as stated on many occasions.

Becca was never more grateful, that she had paid for window tinting on the back of her SUV, virtually making it impossible to see inside.

She made her quick change before they headed out for the second part of their excursion. Cain offered to join her in the back of the roomy Enclave, but she reminded him that's why she needed the cool water in the first place and perhaps they should stick with their plan of joining the others at the Tillamook Creamery.

Cain was all smiles and nodded in agreement.

DUDE... really. DAMN!

A bit of history regarding this very popular dairy establishment.

For instance, did you know it's one hundred and ten years old? Yep, been around since 1909.

Tillamook is proud to have always stood behind the honest values of their farmer-owners. It's from them, the company learned that passion can't be faked, hard work can't be outsmarted, and real food is worth fighting for.

From the farms to their headquarters and from the barns to their creamery... everyone who works for Tillamook has one goal... making the best product out there.

Why else would millions of consumers purchase them, year in and year out.

If you're ever near Tillamook, Oregon be sure and stop by, and check it out for yourself. You won't be disappointed.

By the time Becca and Cain got there, the boys had already started eating the food they had ordered.

Between the four of them, they had fried cheese curds, cheddar cheese fries, grilled cheese sandwiches, Mac n' cheese, something called a Tillamook Madam sandwich that was covered in cheese sauce and a Tillamook eight cheese pizza with copious amounts of meat. It was basically two tables covered in items of cheese with more cheese.

Seriously, makes you feel a tad sorry for their arteries, but everything looked and smelled really wonderful.

Would image it tasted that way as well.

Joel handed Becca a package of zero-sugared peppered jerky he'd gotten at the Smoker's. One of her favorite snacks. Which he discovered by total accident one day when they were shopping at Costco. She'd forgotten she'd even mentioned it; since it was back when they were still in Alaska.

It would seem that Joel doesn't forget much.

So, very thoughtful.

She barely had time to thank him before Cain pulled her towards the restaurant.

Yep, he was hungry.

Becca wasn't surprised when he ordered the Tillamook cheeseburger with a side of cheddar cheese fries, and he actually rolled his eyes when she ordered a salad.

'Hey, it had cheese on it… so suck it up.' Thinking snarky thoughts was always safest.

They joined the others once they had their food and with some strong insistence, she tried the fried cheese curds and one cheesy fry. Both were quite tasty, but she passed on anymore. Even after Cain told her that he'd be happy to help her work off any extra calories she consumed.

Huge fucking blush since he wasn't quiet about the offer.

Frank just shook his head, Joel and Steve both chuckled and the 'Kid' just looked confused which made Becca laugh.

Sometimes youth is totally wasted on the young.

After they all finished their early dinner, the five gentlemen made their way over to the ice cream section for some dessert, and Becca headed to the gift area.

Places that pride themselves on natural ingredients rarely carry a sugar free option. Plus, she was beyond full. And despite what both Joel and Cain thought... she didn't feel that, she needed or wanted any extra calories. And, she had jerky for later.

Cain told her he'd join her in a few minutes and gave her a very 'G' rated kiss.

As she walked away, she couldn't' help but wonder... 'where the hell do they put all that food? And not one of them had a weight issue.' She really should hate them all.

Of course, that made her think of her nephew Jake and his best friend Justin... now, those boys could eat... might even give these gentlemen some serious competition. That thought made her smile. She loved those boys. Well, men actually but since she'd watched them both grow up, she figured she could still call them whatever the hell she wanted.

Back to the here and now.

Becca was just happy that the new jeans she'd gotten just a little over a month earlier were actually a bit loose now; so, she decided not to care what all the men in her life wanted to consume. They could and should eat whatever they wanted.

Who was she to judge?

She was beyond thrilled that she'd not gained any weight after the food police started monitoring her intake and increased it by like ten-fold.

Still though, her numbers were good and she felt great. She really owed both Joel and Cain a huge thank you for her good health.

After several minutes of browsing Becca didn't really find anything that she needed or wanted and started to wander around the rest of the store.

She found pre-wrapped fudge and thought of Cain but decided it wouldn't be as good as the stuff he got in Alaska but if he found it on his own and wanted some, that would be different.

She was surprised; they had a sugar free fudge but it wasn't at all appealing.

Come to think of it… she never did eat the sugar free white chocolate almond bark that Cain had bought for her in Juneau. She wondered what happened to it. She'd have to ask.

Around the next corner she found an amazing assortment of cheese curds in quite of few flavors.

You can even sample most of them if you wish.

She tried a bite of the 'pepper jack habanero' and was very pleased with the spicy morsel. She liked it much better than the fried version she tried earlier.

Joel was there as well and had six packages already in his cart along with four quarts of ice cream and some butter. When he saw the one, she sampled he grabbed a package of those as well and gave her a wink.

She imagined these items would be appearing over the next few days on the yacht's menu. He was in his element. The boy loved to shop.

She also liked the thought that everyone would be heading back to the yacht soon; since ice cream and warm temperatures don't get along that well. She was getting tired.

Steve joined them a minute later with a few more items and Becca took her leave.

'Such a cute couple', she couldn't help but smile.

Cain found her sitting at one of the tables.

Not really a fan of shopping anyway; she decided to just sit and wait for the others.

"You didn't find anything you wanted?" He was just finishing up his bowl of ice cream as he sat down next to her.

She shook her head and smiled at her handsome companion.

He offered her a bite which she declined.

"Baby, one bite of ice cream isn't going to hurt you and mess with your numbers. You're doing so great, and you've lost even more weight since we left for Alaska." He held the spoon to her lips.

She rolled her eyes and got a smirk from Cain.

She took a taste of the Oregon Strawberry; which was very good but refused a bite of the white chocolate raspberry which was his second scoop.

Speaking of white chocolate.

"Do you know whatever happened to that almond bark you bought me?" He laughed and told her that the 'kid' ate it by mistake and was quite regular for two days after. That made them both have a laugh at poor Kevin's expense.

Some sugar free items can cause a laxative effect if you're not careful how much you consume, especially if you're not used to the alternative ingredients used to sweeten certain confections.

Lesson learned apparently.

Cain made short work of the last couple bites of his ice cream.

He did suggest buying another pint to pour on her while they were in bed later.

She still regretted reading him those damn books.

Now if you're wondering which books, you've not been paying attention or didn't read book one, shame on you

Thank God she was done with the punishment reading and got to move on to 'Treasure Island'.

She looked at him and in a very serious tone. "Sticky. So, no." And with that she got up to leave.

He grabbed her hand, and stood to walk out with her.

"Baby, that's what showers or, better yet, jetted tubs are for" and winked.

Of course, she blushed. Hell, I did, and I wrote the damn line.

Joel was through checkout with his bags of goodies and told everyone that he needed to get back to the boat.

Once back at the marina, the 'kid' took Frank's keys and Cain gave Steve back Becca's so they could continue their road trip south.

Frank, Cain and Becca boarded the launch with all the purchases and gave Joel and Steve a little privacy to say their good-byes.

Twenty minutes later all four were back aboard 'SIRA' and everyone went about their duties as if nothing new had happened.

Joel made a dash for the galley with his now melting ice cream and Cain and Frank got the launch stowed.

No huge surprise that the whole boat looked immaculate. Stella was a force to be sure.

Shortly after the launch was put to bed, the captain fired up the engines to take 'SIRA' back out to the open waters of the Pacific Ocean.

Cain yawned a few times on the way back from their outing and went to lay down after helping Frank.

Becca joined him in their stateroom. She was tired but not sleepy.

While he slept, and after she hung up their wet suits in the shower, she Googled the Smokers where her jerky came from since she didn't actually have a chance to go there.

Unlike its big sister... the Tillamook Country Smoker had only been around since the mid '70's.

The original creation was from the Crossley's, a father and son, who built a makeshift smoker in their back yard in the '60's.

They just wanted to create a more delicious jerky using better quality meats. Success! And then some.

A few years later they joined forces with two local farming families, the Smiths and the Geingers and with one handshake, one store and one state they set to put their amazing products in the hands of everyone across America.

Throughout the '80's and '90's, the Tillamook Country Smoker took off and today people who know their products... know they are the best.

Mr. Crossley passed away, but his makeshift smoker is preserved and on display as a memorial tribute to his innovated thinking.

Becca felt a bit sad she didn't get to stop by and visit a place with such a wonderful history.

Maybe she and Cain could take a road trip one day and go back to see everything they missed. Spend a few days instead of only a few hours.

It's funny how she always thinks of them as 'one' when looking at the future.

But isn't that how it's supposed to be when you're in love.

She smiled and opened up her library app to do a bit of reading while her 'love' was napping. She also opened her jerky and snacked on half the bag. 'Damn that's good.'

Cain never stirred and actually slept through the night.

Becca only made it through two and a half chapters of the new JR Rain book before she gave up.

She changed into her nightgown, brushed her teeth and joined her handsome man for an early night of much needed rest.

As always, he instinctively knew when she came to bed and encased her in his arms.

Her most cherished place to be.

WEDNESDAY

When she woke, he was sitting on the bed and looking at her.

He was showered and dressed.

"Morning babe. I was going to leave you a note but watching you sleep is a beautiful treat. Stay in bed as long as you want, and I'll see you in a little while for coffee." He gave her a nice kiss and left.

As Becca was laying there, she was thinking about the lovely time they'd had the day before.

She really did miss swimming... she would thank Cain again for arranging their day trip.

But first a shower and some clothes were the order of the morning.

She thanked Cain again for the amazing day in Oregon while they were having coffee. He finally told her to stop.

He enjoyed it as much as she did.

A little too much since he was still full from his overindulgences.

Once he finished his coffee and declined breakfast, he headed into his office letting her know that he would see her for lunch.

She could tell that something was still bothering him but he wasn't ready to share.

She also knew from experience that he'd reveal his thoughts in his own sweet time, and it had nothing to do with their relationship.

Her sore ass from two weeks prior was a good reminder not to over think.

After she finished another nice light breakfast, she took this alone time to emailed her nephew Jake a nice long letter. She'd not seen him in over six months and after that weird dream and thinking about him yesterday, she really wanted to reach out to him.

Becca told him all about her trip to Alaska and the new man in her life, she even included a picture of she and Cain on deck while they were in Glacier Bay National Park.

Joel had taken it and sent it to her just a few days prior.

She usually hated pictures of herself but to her surprise, she looked pretty good, and Cain look absolutely stunning.

For the very first time in her life, she thought that they made a handsome couple.

If you're wondering why she'd not seen her favorite nephew, all will be revealed in its own sweet time.

She also took time and touched base with Mary again via email regarding any problems with her

Nevada residence and of course, any bills that needed her attention.

Cain had set up autopay for the monthly ones but there seemed to always be one or two that could be missed if she wasn't diligent.

And since her mail hold was up, her very best friend in the universe was indeed keeping tabs on any and all correspondence that might need her attention.

Mary had gotten the post office to put a hold on the mail for an extra few weeks but that was all they were willing to do so; she was collecting it until Becca returned.

Mary got a phone call a week or so back and they told her that she needed to start picking up the mail or they'd deliver to the residence. She opted to pick it up; since she worked about two blocks from the Post Office.

Becca included the same photo of she and Cain in that email as well.

After finishing her main purpose for going into her Hotmail account, she decided it was time to delete the crap load of spam that had accumulated in her under used email, she also saw one from the transcription company she worked for before she took her hiatus.

They sent her a letter to inform her that her services were no longer needed.

'Well, that sucks out loud... but who can blame them.' The thought made her shrug and was a tad upsetting and also made her a little sad.

No one likes to get fired but being totally honest with herself, she never really liked the job anyway, boring to nth degree.

'I'll get another job. Maybe working with Mary', now that thought made her smile.

Becca was eating one of Joel's signature Caesar salads when Cain joined her in the galley. He took a bottle of water from the fridge and again declined food.

He then asked Becca to come find him when she was done eating.

A quick peck on her cheek, and he headed back into his office.

She wasn't sure if she was still hungry since her curiosity was peaked.

Joel gave her that look, the one that told her to please finish her meal and don't stress.

Oh yeah... still one of the wardens of food intake but sweet and caring at the same time.

As mentioned earlier, she didn't have low numbers anymore and was in fact feeling much healthier.

She owed a lot of that to Joel and to Cain.

Still hated being watched and monitored all the time though.

She managed two-thirds with an approving nod from Joel.

He knew that Cain's mood affected everyone on the boat. Especially Becca's.

She went to brush her teeth before going to find out what Cain might want to see her about.

He looked so serious behind his desk but after she entered his domain he put on her smile.

He came around the desk and took her hand leading her over to the couch.

Yep, the one they christened twice, if memory serves.

Thank goodness leather is very forgiving.

Without any preamble, "I was thinking earlier that we haven't really talked much about family and I would like to spend the afternoon doing just that if you're amenable?" His look was inquisitive.

She nodded since she was wondering a few things herself.

"Ladies first babe." And he kissed the ring he moved onto her left hand just a week earlier.

WOW! Just a week. Seems so much longer.

Not to be distracted. Becca started her questions. "I was sort of wondering about lifejackets and your obsession about them? Also, are your folks alive, do you have any siblings, and what is your middle name. We've talked so much about so many things... I'm not sure why after all this time we've never really talked about this stuff." She was smiling at him.

"My thoughts exactly babe. Well, my middle name is Cain, Benjamin Cain Curtis and my twin brother was named Franklin Abel Curtis. My father was and is still a huge fan of the inventor and statesman and my mother is very religious... so they compromised. And yes, Robert and Mabel are both alive and living in San

Antonio, Texas." He stroked her cheek before continuing.

"I was pretty young when I decided I didn't like being called Ben or Benny, so I refused to answer to anything but Cain. Frank didn't seem to mind his first name and never went by Abel which in hindsight was for the best. He drowned in the Gulf of Mexico when we were both fifteen."

The sadness in his eyes made Becca wish, she'd never asked since it was causing him to remember something that was very painful for him.

He gave her a reassuring kiss before continuing his story. "We were sailing in weather that was at best, bad. Hurricane Andrew was heading right for the Gulf, and we were stupid and didn't even check the forecast. It was sunny and the winds were strong so all we thought about was how sailing would be great... we were dumb headstrong teenagers and decided we'd get in one more sail before school started. It went bad quick, and we flipped the boat. Frank wasn't wearing his lifejacket and I was, so I got rescued by the Coast Guard, and they never found my brother. The Gulf took him. I never went near the water again for almost seven years." He paused for a sip of water.

"That's when I met another Frank, in college. It was like some power knew, I needed him in my life, and we became best friends almost immediately. It was Frank Evans who brought me back to the water. So, because of that horrible day, I now need everyone I love to wear a lifejacket." He closed his eyes for a few minutes to reflect on that very personal narrative.

"I'm so sorry Cain." She didn't know what else to say.

"Long time ago baby. You know my mother still blames me, since Cain killed Abel in the bible. She figures there has to be more to the story. We don't talk much, and I haven't gone for a visit in over two years.

I do talk to dad every few weeks. He's going to love meeting you." His smile never reached his eyes, and he gave Becca another nice kiss.

That pretty much let her know that he was done talking but his last statement made her wonder if he'd actually told his father about their relationship, for another time, Cain interrupted her thoughts.

"Your turn Becca. You never talk much about your brother or his family. Let's start there." He had her nestled in the crook of his arm.

"Well, James runs a construction company in Billings Montana and has been married three times, none lasted so he's now giving bachelorhood a try. He likes woman, a lot, sort of a hound dog actually." That made her smile.

"He had his two kids with his second wife Laura but when the boys were young, she decided motherhood wasn't her thing and walked out on them." She was shaking her head at the memory.

"His third wife Rhonda made a great stepmom for the boys but when James moved his company from

Idaho to Montana after his youngest graduated from high school, she didn't go. From my understanding there was quite a bit more to that story, but James has never offered to tell me, and I've never asked. Not really my business." She paused for brief moment.

"My oldest nephew is Mark, he's a dentist and married to Amy. They have three kids, Ashley, Collin and Gail. We're not very close, never have been but it got worse once he got married. His younger brother is Jacob. He only goes by Jake, and he's with the sheriff's department. Single and loving it and he and I have a much stronger bond, always have actually. His partner and best buddy Justin is more like James' third son and my adopted nephew. He grew up with the boys and spent more time at their house and mine than his own. He got dealt a rough hand early on but turned his life around. He's an amazing young man. I have lovingly called he and Jake, JJ, since they were little."

Jake always brought a smile to her face. She loved the little shit. Justin too for that matter.

"If you're wondering why, you never saw any of them at the cabin, it's because I asked them to stay away and let me grieve in peace. Maybe not so much grieve but refocus my life. My brother, along with his oldest and I had a falling out a couple years ago and I am very good at holding grudges. Plus, the summer months are James' busiest with new construction and all… so, it wasn't that big of an ask. Except for Jake." Her expression showed her own bit of sadness.

"Babe, you know I'm not letting that one go, not without a bit more explanation. What was the falling out about?" He repositioned her so he could look at her face better.

She looked away and he could tell she wished she'd never said anything about that part of her life.

"Becca, please. You know how much I love your honesty and seriously, it can't be any worse than my own mother thinking I killed my twin brother." He stroked her face.

He of course was right but to her it all seemed so trivial in comparison.

She sighed. "It's just so utterly stupid, can't we just move on?"

He gave her a firm shake of his head.

"Yep, thought you might not let this go." She looked down at his hand holding hers. He gave it a tender squeeze.

"Okay... so, Mark's wife Amy and I don't get along. You might say we actually detest each other. And when their two oldest used to come out to visit me every summer, Mark brought them out alone or Jake would bring them. Just like James and I and Mark and Jake; Ashley and Collin loved the cabin and they have been swimming in that lake since they were toddlers. It's a great place to be a kid. And it doesn't suck as an adult either." She smiled.

"Anyway, the trip two years ago was different, he brought his wife along and I really did try to be cordial...

for Mark and the kid's sake. Plus, James had made the eight-hour drive over to spend the weekend so he and I could have a chance to visit; and of course, he loved spending time with his grandkids." She paused for her own drink of water.

"That year like the three years prior, I made the trip north from the Nevada property alone for my three weeks stay at the lake. Gary, my late husband, couldn't' take the drive anymore. And as I told you before, it wasn't a happy marriage and truthfully, I relished the break." She paused and took a slight veer from her tale.

"You know, I always thought you shouldn't bail when the going gets tough. But, in retrospection, it might have been better for all concerned if we had divorced years earlier." Sadness reached her eyes and Cain pulled her into his arms. She took a quiet moment enjoying his embrace before continuing.

"It was a nice hot summer day, and the kids were swimming, as usual... all except for Gail, she was only two and a half at the time and Amy wouldn't' let her near the water. For whatever reason Mark never insisted she learn to swim. When it came to Gail, Amy was in complete charge.

I was swimming with the other two and having a really nice time, so I decided to ask Amy if I could bring Gail into the water with me. Just to cool off since it really was a warm day." She made an audible sigh.

"I was given a very firm and resounding 'No' by the child's overprotective mother."

Little side note: Amy couldn't swim very well and never went above her knees into the lake. Probably the reason she wouldn't' let Gail swim.

"Well, since it wasn't my child and wasn't my place to argue with the wretched woman, I shook it off and went back to playing with my other great niece and nephew." She had a very faraway look.

You know the kind, when you're remembering a fond memory or one not so pleasant.

Cain gave her a tender kiss to bring her back to him.

She sighed again. "It was like a minute later that she announced they were leaving and told Mark, who had been in the cabin with his dad, to get the kids ready to go. She informed both men that I was rude and cursed at her because she wouldn't' let me force Gail into the water. And went so far as to tell them that I had scared Gail so badly that she cried." She again shook her head.

"Of course, the entire story was total bullshit, and I didn't do anything she claimed, but both Mark and James believed her without even hearing my side of the story. Hell, even when the other two kids tried to tell their dad and grandpa that I hadn't done anything... they were dismissed, ushered out of the water and up to their car to head home. The only one they believed was that fucking lying bitch." She paused with a very angry look in her eyes.

"I think what really hurt was that my brother would actually think I'd deliberately scare my great niece and refused to discuss it with me, even after everyone had left. He just informed me he would be leaving in the morning. I heard his truck start at the crack of dawn without so much as a 'kiss my ass'." The event still made her sad but pissed her off more.

"We didn't speak again until after Gary died. Which wouldn't' have happened at all if his youngest son hadn't blabbed to him about the death. Jake wasn't there that day, but he took my side because he'd seen how Amy manipulates his brother. That of course caused a huge rift with he and Mark, which I didn't want or mean for that to happen.

But they are grown men. Jake and his dad seem to be fine." That made her chuckle.

"Jake really is the peacekeeper in the family. And my favorite. I know you're not supposed to say that… but it's the truth." She smiled.

"Anyway, it's still a very strained relationship with my brother and I haven't spoken or seen Mark since that day and don't plan to. I do get an email from Ashley once in a while. That does make me sad. It wasn't her fault and still she's collateral damage in the whole situation. I still never miss sending the kids birthday and Christmas gifts." Her expression wasn't total anger, there was still a bit of hurt in the background.

Cain finally interjected. "Firstly, I'm going to let the 'f' bomb slide since it was emotional for you. Secondly, I think you should make up with your brother. He's your kin and I can tell that you miss him in your life." His look was thoughtful.

She shrugged and told him 'Maybe... one day' and then tried to rise from the couch.

Cain pulled her back into his arms with a small head shake.

"I'm very serious about this Becca. Please make peace with your brother and your nephew. Life is too short. Besides, holding grudges is a bit childish." He raised his eyebrows like he was scolding someone much younger.

She was well aware that it was petty and sophomoric but their dismissal of her without so much as listening to her side was beyond hurtful and in her eyes unforgiveable.

She did miss her brother, but truth be told she missed Jake the most. Justin too. And of course, Ashley and Collin, those two kids reminded her so much of she and James growing up at the cabin. Jake and Justin too. Mark, not so much really. And because of his stupid wife, she'd never really gotten to know her youngest great-niece Gail.

Still, maybe she could let it go. One day.

Talk about divine intervention.

Becca's phone rang scaring the crap out of her and startling Cain as well.

"It's Jake." She looked at Cain who asked if she'd like him to leave the room to give her some privacy.

She shook her head and answered the phone, putting it on speaker.

"Hey Jakey. Ears burning?"

"Hi Aunt Becs. What?! No. I was going to respond to your email but decided, I needed to hear your voice. I really missed you this summer. And I wanted to know more about the guy in the photo you sent me? And you went to Alaska?"

"Yes, I did, and it was amazing. I miss you too Jake. His name is Cain, like I told you and he's sitting here listening. Say hello." She smiled.

"Well, that's not awkward, thanks Becca." He sighed before continuing. "HI Cain. I'm Jake Sims the crazy woman's nephew."

Cain grinned. He liked Jake right off. "Hi Jake, it's nice to talk to you. I'm sorry we didn't have a chance to meet in person while I was visiting your beautiful lake."

"That would have been better. But since I have you both on the line, maybe you can convince my stubborn aunt to come to a surprise birthday party I'm throwing for my Pops over Labor Day weekend. The party is a week from this Sunday. He's turning sixty this year. It will be at the cabin, and it won't be any kind of celebration without you there Becca."

Before she even had a chance to respond to his invitation, Cain informed him that they would be delighted to attend the party.

She looked at him with a 'you're in so much fucking trouble' expression since he was way overstepping.

"Listen Jakey... can you email me all the details and I'll get back to you about logistics. I love you boy."

"Love you too and thanks... nice meeting you Cain. See you both very soon."

With that the phone went silent on both ends.

"Don't be mad at me. I'll be there to buffer your re-entry into the family. Besides, you don't want to miss out on your brother's sixtieth." He was wearing her smile.

She didn't want to fight but wasn't he being a bit of a hypocrite. Maybe he should get his own house in order as well. Like going and seeing his mother for starters.

Becca just nodded instead of opening that can of worms.

Thinking they were done, she tried to get up for the second time, but he pulled her back into his arms.

He closed his eyes and gave his own audible sigh.

Apparently, he had something else to say.

'Okay'.

He gave her a quick kiss before starting. "One of the calls I got Monday morning was from my parent company. It would seem that two of my newer clients feel that I've not been doing a good enough job for them and have asked for another advisor. It happens on occasion, but I've never had it happen to me, so I was really shocked.

I vet my clients carefully, so this kind of thing doesn't happen." He took another sip of water.

"Anyway, they have gone so far as to file a formal complaint against me as well. Because of that stunt, I've been summoned to the main headquarters in New York for a sit down with my boss and the HR department to determine if I'm still a good fit for the company." He took a deep breath and continued.

"The reason this is so huge for me; is that I am in fact, the only employee they have, that works solely in a remote setting without a physical office." He paused for another second.

"Because of these circumstances, the next several days I'm going to be very busy compiling affidavits from my clients who might want to leave if I'm let go. It will be my safety net... just a precaution, if this meeting doesn't go well."

This time Becca squeezed his hand to bring him back to her.

"I've made this company a lot of money over the years and I'm more than surprised by this turn of events considering my track record, but with social media and everything else, these two individuals can cause some serious damage and not just for me. So, that's why I required some major distraction the other day. I needed time to wrap my head around what might happen if I'm asked to resign." He just shook his head.

"So, again, I want to thank you for being here. And to let you know how much I love you Becca and how blessed I feel that you are in my life, and I hope you're ready to ride out this storm with me." He gave her a very tender kiss.

"Cain, I love you with every fiber of my being so yes, I will be here, always, no matter what happens in our life. Now, tell me how I can help?" She was so glad he finally confided in her.

"Becca, I would like to hire you to type the transcripts I'll need for each of the affidavits I'm able to get. I'm sure there will be other items that will need to be typed, formatted and notarized but we can take things one step at a time. Say twenty-five dollars an hour." He had on his business persona.

She had to think about that for a few minutes. On one hand she did just get fired earlier in the day and could use the income, but she was sleeping with Cain and having him as her boss and her lover seemed wrong on quite a few levels. Plus, that was an insane amount of money for just a bit of typing.

And as you're probably aware, he still sucks when it comes to compromise.

But being forever hopeful she ploughed ahead with her suggestion.

"How about I just do the typing and you can keep your money until you're sure you are gainfully employed. Both of us can't be out of work after all." She smiled at him.

"What do you mean both of us out of work? Did you quit your job?" No smiles with his inquiry.

In fact, it sounded a tad accusatory!

Well, that changed the mood of the conversation rather quickly.

"No! I did not quit. Thank you very much. I was fired via email earlier today." She moved one cushion down on the couch, so they were no longer touching.

"And you kept this information from me, why?" He actually looked miffed

Why yes, his attitude pissed her off. Wouldn't it you?

"As I just stated. I found out today and I've just not had the opportunity to tell you. What with everything else we've been discussing." Her tone indicated that she was so done talking to him.

This time she stood and made it out the study door without giving him a single glace and didn't give a crap about his response. She didn't quite slam the door, but it shut with more force than it needed.

Does anyone else think she really should have been born a red head with that temper of hers. Just saying.

Becca walked out of the main salon and up one flight of stairs towards her final destination, the front seating area where she and Cain had sunbathed just over six short weeks ago.

Wow! Time flies.

It was sunny and warm but the wind on the Pacific was a bit brisk.

She didn't care... she was totally hacked and just needed to put some distance between them so she could settle down.

Her phone rang again, and it was Jake.

She took a cleansing breath before answering. "Hey Jake... yeah I'll come... no that pretty much pissed me off... it just happened... you had to have seen his fucking huge ass yacht on the lake, the damn thing is over a hundred feet with the name 'SIRA' emblazoned on the stern... you're kidding, you're the one who threatened to ticket the boat unless it moved... small world... yep that's what I'm currently on just south of Coos Bay heading to San Diego... no... I will not call your fucking brother... don't push it Jake or you'll lose out on my half of the cabin... I still may leave it to the 'flat earth society'... boy don't push your luck or you'll see every naked baby picture I have of you on 'Facebook' on your next birthday... good decision... tell Justin I say 'hi' back... yes.. you too."

She really did love the little shit.

After she hung up from her call with her nephew, she noticed Cain was watching her.

Still irked at him. "Eavesdrop much?!"

He shook his head and sat down next to her on the lounge chair.

"Please stop being angry at me." His look was hopeful.

"I'm sorry about my reaction to your news. I'm also sorry that you lost your job because of me. And I didn't mean to intrude on your conversation, but I do love the way you interact with your nephew. I can tell how much you love him and damn, you really put him in his place." He took her hand and brought it to his lips.

She really can't stay mad at him.

Something he was well aware of.

"Now, can we get back to discussing you working for me?"

Like a dog with a bone, he just doesn't let things go. 'Fine then'. She smirked at him and said, "I'll take thirty dollars an hour."

He laughed and asked if she'd take partial payment in trade.

She couldn't' help but laugh as well.

Bad mood totally thwarted.

Well played Mr. Cain.

She made note that he let her two 'f' bombs while talking to Jake slide without mention.

Smart man.

They laid on the chaise lounge for another twenty minutes or so, just being close and enjoying the quiet.

Neither spoke during that span, and it was cathartic for them both.

When Joel showed up with afternoon smoothies, they both jumped since it was totally unexpected. They hadn't worked up any kind of appetite.

Becca made another observation; Cain's glass was actually the same size as hers this time and they were almost the same color. That's new.

Joel handed Becca the one with the pink straw and Cain got one with a clear straw... good way to tell which was which.

He got huge smiles and thank yous from them both.

As it turns out, Becca got a smoothie while Cain got a milkshake.

Yep, Tillamook's finest.

"I need to give that man a raise." Cain finished his shake in record time.

Without missing a beat. "Maybe he'll take it in trade?" Becca raised her eyebrow at him and smiled.

For once he wasn't drinking anything... the comment totally caught him off guard.

His expression made her laugh.

He took her glass and put it on the deck next to his and almost growled telling her she might want to run.

She did.

Amazingly enough she managed to evade him for almost an hour by hiding in plain sight. Back on the same lounge chair they'd both been on earlier.

"There you are my clever girl," and he held out his hand for her to take. He could feel the chill on her skin, and shook his head. "Let's get you into a warm shower before dinner."

The warm water felt wonderful, but Cain washing her hair was the real pleasurable experience. She looked forward to their showers together, and she had to admit that it was actually sad for her when she bathed alone.

"I cherish these moments with you. And I wanted you to know that." She turned and gave him a kiss before rinsing the shampoo out of her hair. He pulled her back to his lips for a very intimate kiss. A whispered in her ear, "Baby, I adore everything we do together.

Including an argument or two." He pressed against her letting her know his intentions.

Yep, they had to reheat dinner. Total shocker, not.

While they were enjoying their late evening supper, the captain came in to talk with Cain.

A rarity.

He did seem quite concerned about some weather heading their way.

Cain excused himself and headed to the bridge once his engineer who also happened to be his best friend joined them.

Now it was Becca's turn to be concerned.

Evidently the typhoon that had disrupted their voyage into Northern Alaska had finally made its way south and was about to become a nuisance once again.

With high wind alerts and small craft warnings going out from the Coast Guard, the decision was made by Cain, Frank and the Captain to run throughout the night at ten to twelve knots and try to maintain that speed so they could reach San Francisco Bay as soon as possible. Once there, they would be able to ride out the storm moored at South Beach Harbor.

Not being the captain's first storm, he had already radioed ahead to reserve a space since there weren't that many harbors that could accommodate the one-hundred-foot yacht. Plus, Cain didn't want to even try to anchor, it would be too hard to keep the big boat in place with the strong currents and winds.

The three men would all be on the bridge taking shifts throughout the night and into the next day. Not only watching weather and waves but keeping their eyes peeled for other smaller boats and any debris that could damage the yachts hull.

They had in fact topped off the tanks at Coos Bay at four that morning just like Cain told Becca they would and reaching the Bay area was usually just over a day's journey, but they were going a bit slower due to the rougher seas.

Truth be told, she hadn't even realized that the seas were that chopping although she had felt the wind while on deck earlier in the day.

They were in California waters at least and had been for the last couple hours so Cain thought it was doable to make the harbor just before noon the next day.

THURSDAY - Early

Joel, Becca and Stella were on coffee delivery duty, since no one seemed to like the idea of sleeping. Well almost no one.

Frank took his break around three in the morning and crashed in the smaller guest room one floor below the bridge not wanting to be too far away if needed.

About that same time, Becca was bringing the gentlemen more coffee and fresh muffins, when she found out the threesome were down to a duo.

"Babe, I appreciate you keeping us plied with sugar and caffeine, but I would like you to go lay down for a few hours please." Cain could tell she was exhausted.

Weren't they all?

She shook her head and told him that she would sleep when he did. She also told him to suck it up and eat his muffin. In turn he gave her a rather stern look.

That got a chuckle from Larry since he was married to a rather stubborn woman himself.

Cain raised his eyebrow letting her know that she might want to leave.

She gave him a quick kiss and left the bridge.

The winds had increased throughout the early morning hours, which caused the yacht to slow its speed, making everyone feel the ocean's wrath a bit more so, Becca had to hold the railing tight, since the rains had decided to join the party and the steps were now quite slippery.

With the boat rocking a bit more and between the wind and a slick deck from the rain she fell twice.

Overachiever that she is.

Once at the stairway leading down to the main salon, she breathed a sigh of relief... no major injuries... maybe a bruise or two.

However; in that short amount of time, she still managed to get drenched and was now physically cold.

"Miss Becca are you alright? I don't think you should deliver anymore coffee. You either, Stella. I'll take care of it." Joel was looking at her with very concerned eyes.

She told him that she was fine and was going to take a quick shower and put on some dry clothes.

He told her that she should try and lay down for a few hours, but she was having none of that nonsense. She wouldn't do it for Cain, she sure as hell wasn't going to do it for Joel.

But she did ask him to please make her some peppermint tea.

Her stomach was not a fan of the motion of the ocean. 'Crap! Again?'.

Under the warm water of the shower, she felt so much better.

His hands coming around her made her scream.

He didn't apologise.

Cain examined the small red mark on her hip and the one on her elbow.

"You left the bridge to see my little bruises. Don't you have more pressing matters?" She loved his attentiveness but maybe not at that particular moment.

His hand smacked her ass pretty hard.

Don't be daft of course it stung.

Cain turned off the water and handed Becca a towel. She wrapped it around herself and started to dry her hair with a smaller one.

"Good enough." And he took the towel and tossed it on the counter.

He led her back into their stateroom and told her to get into bed.

"You first." She crossed her arms.

He smirked. "Fine" and proceeded to drop his towel from around his waist and climb under the covers.

What an amazing view! Never gets old.

"You joining me or not?" He sounded less stern and patted the bed.

She had a feeling something was up but, she had said she'd sleep if he did. So, following his lead, she let her towel drop on the floor and she crawled under the sheets.

He pulled her into his arms.

"Here. Joel gave me your tea. Drink up so you don't get seasick baby." He handed her the cup from his nightstand.

It smelled wonderful. She loved peppermint and drank the lukewarm beverage in record time.

Nestled into his arms she suddenly felt so very tired.

"Sleep Becca. I love you," was the last thing she remembered hearing.

Peppermint tea is a wonderful remedy for mild cases of seasickness but when you add some liquid Dramamine it works even better.

If you're wondering... Frank heard Becca fall and went and told Cain.

Joel handing him the tea was just perfect timing. And gave him the idea to spike her drink.

Even stubborn women need sleep.

Now... keep that to yourselves since he would be in a 'world of shit' if she ever finds out.

Later that same day -

Becca woke with a major headache and was just a little surprised to see Cain sleeping peacefully next to her.

For some weird reason, she thought he'd only come to bed to get her to sleep.

She tested her numbers, which were normal. That's always good but now, she needed to find some Tylenol and a robe since she was still naked.

Suitably covered she headed to the galley to find a bottle of water.

The main floor was quiet... eerily quiet.

The sun was high in the sky, although covered by clouds, she could see it was early afternoon and not a soul was stirring.

She got her water and took the two lovely pills as she headed to the back deck.

They were safely in the Bay and although it was still blowing and lightly raining the boat wasn't moving much.

They were tied up to the dock.

"Good Job Gentlemen." She saw his reflection in the window so, he didn't scare the hell out of her that time.

"Thank you, babe. Now come back to bed... we only just tied up half hour ago."

He looked like a walking and talking zombie, so Becca helped her very tired man back to bed.

She was almost positive he was asleep before his head hit the pillow.

That confirmed her earlier thought. He had only come to bed previously to get her to sleep.

'What a sweetheart.' She wasn't mad at all.

While Cain and the rest of the very tired crew slept, Becca was wide awake and decided to find something to do.

With IPad in hand she found that she had free Wi-Fi. SCORE!

She decided to stay in bed next to her man so, he would sleep and searched online for a place around the harbor area to go and grab everyone dinner.

Since South Beach Harbor was near the neighborhoods of China Basin and next to Mission Bay, there were hundreds of food choices and all within a mile or two.

Becca calculated that everyone would sleep for five to six hours giving her plenty of time to order and pick-up food.

They hadn't had Chinese food since she'd been aboard the boat so, she hoped that everyone would like her choice.

Twenty-five websites later and feeling a tad overwhelmed, she decided on 'Jade Cafe'. It was one of the farthest at two point three miles, but it had the best prices and tons of choices.

That killed a little over an hour of time.

She figured she could walk to the restaurant and order the food and get a cab back to the harbor.

Now she wondered just how pissed off Cain would be if she bought dinner again?

She could wake Joel but that somehow defeated the purpose of letting the exhausted crew get some well-deserved rest.

Cain's breathing was deeper now, so she knew it was safe to move.

She took a very quick shower, since her hair was a fright from sleeping on it wet, then got dressed in jeans and a warm sweater.

She still had a slight headache and really wanted coffee.

Sitting at the galley counter, Becca ate a yogurt after her second cup of coffee and was still debating how to broach her dinner idea with just a note when the stairway door opened.

She was only mildly startled.

Joel emerged looking half awake.

"Why are you up? Go back to your room and sleep for another hour or two."

'Oh my God, I sound like my mother'. She smiled at the thought.

"Good Afternoon to you too Miss Becca. And if you must know, I went to bed two hours after you did. Mr. Cain's orders." He smiled at her.

'Fifty was still a very good nickname for him, what with his control freakishness.' Just one that she'd never say out loud again... ever. She chuckled at the thought.

She was actually quite happy to see Joel since he could now be her sounding board for her dinner idea.

"Can I get you a cup of coffee for a change." She grinned at him.

He laughed. "No ma'am"

Becca knew she was fifteen-plus years older than him, but she hated being called 'ma'am'. So matronly.

"Miss Becca, if you're planning something clever to say please wait until I have a Coke. My brain is still catching a few extra zees."

Well, that lightened the mood. And she laughed.

"I was thinking about dinner and wondering what you might think of ordering Chinese food for everyone?"

She smiled since she remembered the last-time she suggested ordering dinner. Oops.

"I found a place about two miles away that looks very promising. It's called the 'Jade Cafe'." She waited for him to take a drink of his Coca-Cola.

Joel just nodded his approval.

Good Man!

"Should we test Cain's temper and have me pay again?" Her grin was a bit evil.

"NO! I'll pay... please. I can't go through that again. Really." His pensive look made her laugh for a second time.

"You do know that I never meant for you to get into trouble." She really was sorry that Cain lectured him about his duties, twice.

Joel nodded and smiled.

"Where do you think Steve and the 'Kid' are? I was thinking of walking there and grabbing a cab on the return trip but if we have vehicles in the area... that would be even better." She barely had time to finish her question and Joel was on his phone.

"Hi honey, where are you? Really... San Francisco." He gave Becca a huge grin and winked.

"We're here too... yeah... the storm brought us into South Beach Harbor... oh fuck, really... no, I'm not telling him... nope, not going to happen... yes, come here... you and the 'Kid' can stay on the yacht tonight... he'll have to face the music himself... love you and I'll see you soon." And with that, his call was done but Becca had many questions.

Her quizzical look told him to spill without her uttering one word.

"It would seem that the 'kid' got in a small accident. No one's hurt except for Frank's SUV. And before you ask... yes, it was his fault, and he has the ticket to prove it. He was going too fast and clipped a Dodge Ram on slick roads. The SUV is getting repaired, but it will take another day maybe two." Joel shook his head.

"Oh fuck, that's bad on so many levels." And she felt sort of sorry for the 'kid' since Frank was going to lose his shit. He loved that car.

"Becca! You know I hate you saying that word." Cain was up.

Both she and Joel jumped since neither of them had noticed his arrival.

"Damn, you're stealthy. Why are you up so early?" Deciding to just ignore his irritation regarding the use of the 'f' word.

She also took note while glancing at the clock in the living room, he'd only been asleep around three and a half hours.

He went and retrieved a bottle of water before holding his hand out to her and giving his chef a nod.

She shrugged at Joel, since she knew better than to argue and left the main salon with Cain and returned to their room.

"Come and lay down with me." Becca could tell that he was still worn out and needed more rest.

She removed her tennis shoes and climbed into bed with him.

He shook his head. "Clothes off."

"Cain, Joel and I are going to go pick up dinner for everyone in about an hour. So, how about I just lay here until you go back to sleep."

His look was pure evil, and he proceeded to wrap his arms around her ensuring that she wasn't going anywhere without having to wake him up first.

Great!

So, now with the covers and his body heat, she was in fact way over dressed.

'Fuck'.

Thinking it shouldn't count.

She was happy her phone was in her pocket, and she managed to pull it out without too much difficulty and without waking Cain.

She sent Joel a text to let him know that he was on his own and he'd find the 'Jade Cafe' on Bryant Street.

He sent her back a 'thumbs up' emoji.

Now she really wished she could reach her IPad, at least then she could read, since she just didn't feel tired enough to sleep but her now comatose octopus was out cold, and his vise grip had her stuck and beyond warm.

Becca settled for playing 'Word-scapes' on her phone until, she was actually tired, and her battery was in the red. She had just closed her eyes when the arms that ensnared her, released her.

She decided to keep her eyes closed and waited for Cain to get up.

Instead, he started to undress her.

His lips were at her ear. "I know you're awake. Arms up baby." She did as he requested, and her sweater was off and discarded somewhere. He also made short work with her bra giving him free reign over her breasts.

Jeans were next.

His attention to detail was incredible. He made short work of getting the girls nice and hard before giving Becca her first climax with just his very clever tongue.

She was in the middle of aftershocks when he filled her and gave her another rather spectacular release. He joined her in the second.

It was clear that he was very well rested.

Becca felt spent. Thoroughly sated but spent.

"You want dessert before dinner my girl?" He was giving her another rather nice kiss.

How could she still be so aroused by him? The moan escaped before she could stop it.

"As you wish." And his kiss intensified and before she knew it, they were having another lovely interlude and the weight of his body on hers felt perfectly wonderful.

Damn she loved this man. But he was seriously trying to kill her with orgasms.

It was full-on dark when Becca woke from their early evening of lovemaking but this time, she was alone.

She could hear voices coming from the living room and dining room but didn't feel like being social at that moment.

Fact is, she always felt self-conscious when she was the last to join in the festivities.

She got up and used the bathroom, found her clothes and took another quick shower before redressing. It was just after nine and it dawned on her that she'd not eaten anything but a yogurt that day. She didn't feel shaky, but she did have another mild headache.

When she came out of the bathroom, Cain was waiting for her.

"I was coming to get you for dinner. Brilliant idea you had ordering Chinese." He pulled her into his arms and gave her one of his amazing hugs.

"Is the 'Kid' still alive or did Frank toss him overboard?" The thought just popped into her mind, and she said it out loud.

"What? Why?" He was beyond confused.

"Nothing." She tried to shrug off her question.
"Becca... please fill in the blanks regarding that rather odd query." He had on his stern face.

"Okay but first tell me where Frank is?"

"He just came up and is fixing himself a plate. The 'Kid' actually left when Frank arrived now that I think about it." He raised his eyebrows to her.

"Frank's SUV was involved in a little accident." And she went to leave.

For a big guy he's really quick.

Becca found herself flat on the bed trapped under Cain.

"More details... now please". He had her totally pinned.

Shit he was serious.

"I don't know that much... ask the 'Kid'... he caused it. That's why he and Steve are still in San Francisco. I thought Joel would fill you in." Yep, she managed to throw everyone under the bus with that explanation.

"Fuck!" He let her up.

"How come when I said that earlier you got all hot and bothered. It was regarding the same information when I heard it?" She was actually glaring at him.

He smirked. "Because I don't want you to. It's more offensive to me when you say it."

"Prude!" And shook her head.

He proceeded to give her a very hard smack on the ass making her jump. He then took her hand in his and they left their room to join the others for dinner.

Frank was finishing up his first plate and heading back for seconds when Cain and Becca joined them.

"What took you two so long?" And he winked at Becca.

Oh, hell no, she wasn't going to put up with any of that.

Looking right at Frank she stated matter-a-factly. "We were discussing the unconventional ways one can use the word 'fuck'."

Cain choked on the water he was attempting to drink.

Joel and Steve both started to laugh.

Frank just nodded.

Without even looking at him, she pulled her hand away from Cain's and went and got a plate.

She did apologize to Stella who waved her off saying it's a fitting word on occasion. Captain Larry patted his wife on the back.

That made Becca smile.

She really did love Chinese food but the amount of MSG and carbs it contained were a dangerous combination so she knew, she'd have to be careful or spend the next day or two on the treadmill.

It was a fine line to manage since she also knew both Cain and Joel, who'd done very well with the selection would be monitoring her intake.

Annoying!

She chose the foil-wrapped chicken since it's usually safe and a little chow mien wouldn't kill her. She also took a couple of scoops of Kung Pao shrimp and Szechwan chicken. She did love spicy.

She grabbed a bottle of water, chopsticks and took a seat at the dining room table across from Frank.

Cain sat down next to her, and it was the first time she noticed the front of his shirt was damp.

Oops. He shook his head at her.

His mood improved instantly when she started to eat.

'Freak!'

"So, Steve, I was just curious what delayed your road trip?" Cain's expression didn't give away anything.

Becca wanted to kick him under the table.

'Fucking Instigator!'

Again, can't get in trouble for thinking it.

Cain raised his eyebrow like he knew she said it in her head.

Well, Hell!

About the time Steve was feeling the pressure to tell the tale. Kevin walked back into the room.

"Mr. Frank, I got in an accident with your SUV and it's currently at the body shop getting a new right front panel and tire. I didn't judge the braking distance in the rain and clipped a Dodge Ram. I'm going to have to pay for his new taillight but that was the only damage to his rig. And I'm covering all the repairs on your ride as well. I'm very sorry." He looked so very young at that moment.

Becca looked at Frank who just shrugged.

"I have insurance, just cover the deductible and that will be fine. Thanks for telling me. The most important thing is that you didn't get hurt 'Kid' or hurt anyone else." And with that, he went back to finishing his dinner.

Cain squeezed Becca's hand and smiled at his friend.

The Abbot's embraced their son, and they all sat on the couch in the living room having a family discussion.

Joel asked if anyone wanted anymore food before he put it away for the night.

No one did.

Steve helped him and they both said their goodnights once finished with that task.

Frank was the next to bid everyone a nice night. The Abbot family followed shortly behind him leaving Cain and Becca alone.

"Did you get enough to eat?"

She nodded

"Are you tired?"

She shook her head

"Not very chatty this evening?"

"Just wondering if you're still miffed, or are we passed the earlier incident?"

"Well, you've been quite sassy this evening, but I sort of love that about you, so I think I'm past it." He smiled.

It was her smile, and she knew everything was good.

Even though she had a nice nap, Cain wanted to get their sleeping pattern back on track and wanted them to turn in.

She ended up reading him four more chapters of 'Treasure Island' that night before drifting off into a blissful slumber in his arms.

FRIDAY

Here's the issue with sleep... once your body has had enough, it wakes its ass up.

Even before the sun on some occasions.

So, just a bit past four-thirty Becca was wide awake.

She managed to get out of bed without disturbing Cain and headed to the galley with her IPad after a quick trip to the bathroom and grabbing her robe.

The coffee that morning tasted amazing, and she decided to sit on the couch while looking for an early morning bakery.

Much more affordable than their dinner from the previous evening, and it shouldn't get someone's hackles up.

Someone being Cain of course.

She figured she'd pushed enough of his buttons yesterday and the day before actually.

'He makes it so easy'. That thought made her smile.

Eureka!

The Bagel Bakery was open at 6 am and was only a ten-minute walk to their Townsend Street location. Perfect.

She'd overheard the captain telling Cain and Frank during dinner that they would be leaving around 7 am to make their fuel time.

Taking on fuel is quite the process for these huge yachts. It can take hours and hours to fill a beast of 'SIRA' size. To fill a Mega Yachts would take almost two days. And cruise ships can take a week and a half to take on fuel.

Her list consisted of Bagels, Cream Cheese and Lox for eight people.

Yes. The woman happens to like lists.

Now to get showered, dressed and leave Cain a note.

She managed everything and all before quarter to six on this lovely morning.

And the best part... she did it all without waking her handsome hunk.

With wallet, list and phone in hand, she placed the note on her pillow and headed towards the stairs and down two flights to the back deck and onto the dock.

She was pleased that no one else seemed to be up quite yet. Perfect.

It really was a gorgeous morning. The sky was blue, and the sun was just making its way to greet the day. The storm had made its point and left to continue its southeastwardly journey.

Becca made it to the bakery just a few minutes after they opened, and she was not even close to being the first in line. San Francisco had many early risers it would seem.

She took her time selecting a nice assortment of Bagels. Some savory and some sweet. She decided on three different s of cream cheese: French Vanilla, Garden Herb and Smoked Gouda. She also got the lox and a small container of capers.

After waiting for them to package everything up and paying, she'd been off the yacht for just under thirty-five minutes. Not bad, but she wanted to hurry back before Joel started to cook breakfast for everyone. And of course, before they cast off.

She was back on the docks ten minutes later but there was only one small issue.

'SIRA' was gone.

"Fuck me! What the hell… it's not 7a yet!" Not a usual habit to vent out loud but she was really hacked.

Becca dropped her bags on the empty dock and reached for her phone.

Cain answered on the first ring.

"Morning... nope... did you see the note I left?" She paused.

It would seem that Stella was coming into his study to hand him the note she had found, as she was changing the sheets on the bed.

"Yep... I'm currently standing on the dock where your yacht used to be."

He was telling her where they were heading with a very stern voice.

"Didn't you wonder at all where I was when you got up?" When he didn't reply, she continued.

"Well, it's handy that you're on your way to Oakland to top off the tanks. What the fuck do you want me to do?" The situation and his tone made her more pissed at that precise moment. She didn't care about her tone or verbiage.

He started his language lecture. She wasn't a fan.

"I couldn't' give a rat's ass if you don't like the word. Get over it."

He apparently didn't like her attitude either.

She stopped listening when he started another language lecture and thought, 'Damn Becs, good deeds and you, totally suck out loud.'

She interrupted him, "where are Steve and the 'Kid'? Are they still on board? If so, where's my car?" She was forming a plan.

She could tell he was walking and talking and refusing to answer her questions, again. She was also pretty sure that he was getting mad at both her and at the situation since the tenor of the conversation was getting elevated.

He was almost yelling that they were never to leave port without doing a head count.

Becca was now listening to Cain converse with the captain at the same volume he had with her.

She was feeling stressed and began to feel like she was eavesdropping on a private conversation, so she hung up.

She did think twice about answering his call but had the good sense to put it on speaker, in case he was yelling. Save her eardrums the wear and tear in the process.

Good Call and wouldn't' you do the same.

"Rebecca Lynne, don't you dare ever hang up on me again. That was rude. I'm trying to arrange for the launch to come back and get you since we'll be in Oakland for several hours taking on fuel. In saying that, you still may be stranded for an hour or two. The captain got offered an earlier fuel time so, he took advantage and didn't think to see, if anyone had left due to the early hour. Plus, I've told you on several occasions to 'NOT LEAVE THE YACHT' without telling me. I guess this will be a damn good lesson." He had the pitch of an angry father.

'Jackass! And she did leave a note. Not her fault he didn't see it.'

She was getting tired of him scolding her and rather than tell him to 'fuck off' she hung up on him, again.

Fiery redhead... you can see it now, can't you?

This time Becca also turned her phone off.

Seriously, what right did Cain have to be all pissed at her, she was the one who had to sit around and wait. And she hated being called Rebecca and throwing in the middle name like, she was an errant child was way over the top.

A thought did pop into her head.

It would seem the ever-resilient Mrs. Jackson had placed a hidden key on her car, and was thinking of retrieving it and driving away. That would only happen if she could actually find her Buick.

It was; after all, a little under ten hours from the coast to her house in Nevada. Or she could call Frank and get the address of the fuel dock and just drive over to Oakland but that meant turning on her phone and that just wasn't going to happen. Plus, she didn't know where her car was actually parked. Definitely not in her line of sight... from any angle.

She knew that she would never drive all the way back to Ely, since she happened to love the 'shithead' that she just hung up on, twice.

Still, the thought made her smile.

Button pusher extraordinaire.

She should have shirts made.

Back to the reality of the situation... 'The wait!' She got as comfortable as she could on the dock to 'veg' out until her ride returned.

She thought of eating a bagel but didn't want to consume that amount of carbs, even if she was getting a mild headache and her stomach growled. Plus, part of her quick temper was more than likely a result of low blood sugars, so yes, she should eat. But stubbornly wouldn't.

'Fuck can't even play games since that would require turning on my phone.' huge sigh.

Forty minutes later she was surprised to see the launch heading her way.

Her instant thought was, 'Shit! That can't be nearly enough time for him to have calmed the hell down'.

You could see her relief when she saw it was Frank, Joel, Steve and Kevin.

'A reprieve. YES!'

"Hey Frank." She smiled at Cain's best friend.

"Becca my dear, you have managed to really rile him up. I've not seen him this angry in quite a while. The only person he didn't snap at this morning was Stella." He was shaking his head at her.

"Maybe it's best if I just take my car and head for Nevada." She winked at Frank.

"Fuck that Miss Becca... I'm not going back without you and face his wrath which will be refocused on Mr. Frank and myself, guaranteed." Joel apparently missed the wink.

She let out a very audible sigh.

"I just wanted to get everyone bagels for breakfast. And I don't want to deal with his anger issues either." She was pouting a bit but knew, she was going back with them.

"Bagels?" The 'Kid's' eyes lit up. That made her chuckle.

She handed him the two bags and boarded the launch.

She laughed when the four men divided up the food.

Steve and the 'Kid' stayed on the dock and were heading to her Enclave while, she and the other two headed back to the boat.

She refused the lifejacket Frank attempted to hand her. And thankfully he didn't push the issue.

"Miss Becca, I'm also supposed to tell you to turn on your phone." Joel shrugged.

She just shook her head. 'Fuck that'.

Truth be told, she wouldn't' have minded dropping the damn thing into San Francisco Bay. But replacing it would be pricey, so she refrained.

'SIRA' came into view way too quickly for her liking. 'JOY.'

The only saving grace was that he wasn't on the lower deck waiting.

Maybe he's busy working in his study. That would be the best-case scenario.

"My dear, just go and find him, please. You'll both be happier once you've made up." Frank had a really nice smile and was truly a good friend to Cain and to her.

She nodded.

She had thoughts of barricading herself in one of the spare rooms until they reached San Diego but that would make her as childish, and he was overbearing.

Putting her big girl panties on, she walked up to the main salon and went and knocked on Cain's office door.

"Come in," nothing in that gave her a clue as to his mood.

She opened the door and went and sat in one of the leather chairs facing his desk.

She didn't smile but looked him right in the eye when she spoke.

"I'm sorry I hung up on your lecture. And you're right, I shouldn't leave the boat without telling you. Thanks for sending Frank to pick me up. That was very thoughtful."

"You're welcome. Thank you for letting me know you're back on board." He paused looking at her.

"I have several calls to make this morning regarding the situation I spoke to you about on Wednesday so why don't we just let this morning's incident go and move on?" He didn't smile either.

She nodded and got up to leave.

"Becca." His tone was much gentler.

She turned, as he was coming from around his desk.

He opened his arms. Becca walked into his embrace.

She hugged him tight because he needed to know how much she hated fighting, and that she loved him so very much.

He tilted her head up to meet his lips.

"I'll see you later for lunch my girl" and he smiled her smile.

She nodded and was leaving his office feeling like the weight of the world was off her shoulders.

Before she had the chance to close the door, Cain made one more statement that caught her totally off guard.

"One more thing babe. If I hear the word 'fuck' coming out of your mouth again, ever. You'll be going over my knee." His look told her he wasn't kidding.

Well, that wasn't so bad... they had worse... well... maybe not.

Even though she showered earlier, she felt gross and went and took another quick rinse. Basically, trying to wash-off the entire early morning fiasco.

Now she needed food and more coffee.

She headed to the galley to find some yogurt or maybe, she could convince Joel to make her a protein drink.

When she sat down, he handed her a cup of coffee and half a toasted bagel with cream cheese and fresh berries.

She wasn't about to argue with anyone else this day and ate her breakfast after thanking the sweet chef.

Joel took the other half and added lox and capers and put it on a tray with a fresh cup of coffee and headed into Cain's study.

He emerged with just the tray.

Again, it's the little things... Becca smiled at the thought of Cain eating what she'd purchases for him, just two hours earlier.

You know, before the shit hit the fan.

After breakfast, she went and changed into workout clothes.

She was still feeling a bit of tension from earlier; plus, she ate a fucking bagel.

Thinking the word doesn't count.

She managed a good forty minutes on the treadmill. A nice accomplishment since the machine let her know she did in fact work off her breakfast and then some.

Of course, now she needed yet another shower.

It was only ten-thirty when she emerged in fresh clothes.

'Now what?'

They would be in Oakland for a couple more hours taking on fuel.

She grabbed her IPad and went and sat in the living room.

Joel wasn't in the galley but would be in another hour or two to start lunch, so she had the salon pretty much to herself.

Cain was there, but he was tucked away in his office working.

Her first thought was to read a few more chapters of the new book, she downloaded but instead went into her email.

She was happy to see a new one had arrived from her nephew Jake.

Dear Aunt Becs,

I went and found the permit for the yacht you told me about. You weren't exaggerating... she's a beast. And I also found out why Cain's name didn't sound familiar... he listed ownership under Benjamin C. Curtis and Franklin D. Evans. Really Becca... Benjamin Franklin... if it was anyone but you, I'd have never believed it and thought someone was pulling a huge scam.

And I was right about me being the one who told them to leave the area by the cabin because of weekend traffic. It didn't dawn on me until you said something... that huge boat was really close to the cabin. It also explains why the two times Justin and I went by to check on you, the cabin was dark, so we didn't stop.

Probably a good thing since there is no way in hell that I want to catch my favorite aunt in the sack with ANYONE!

Although, if memory serves you caught me, twice. Not my finest hour. Either time. And you handled it with your usual wit... thank God. You know Pops would have blown the preverbal gasket. If I'm remembering the details right... you said "Boy, if you're not wearing a raincoat, I'll be cutting it off'.

Fuck, that was too funny.

Also reminds me of the box of condoms you gave me for my 15th birthday. Rhonda was so pissed at you. Pops had a helluva time calming her down. She wanted to ban you from the house. Said you were giving me ideas. Sometimes she wasn't the brightest of individuals. Big heart though.

Sorry for the major detour down memory lane but every memory of you is cherished. You know you really are my favorite aunt, don't you? I figure right about now you're reminding me that you're my only aunt but that isn't the case. I have two on my mom's side... I just don't associate with them.

You're rolling your eyes at me now, I would guess.

I miss you so much Becca.

Anyway... the two real reasons for this long-ass email,

I wanted to reiterate how important it is that you attend Pops 60th birthday bash at the cabin. I was serious, you have to be there. He needs to see you, and he really needs for you to forgive him. Please trust me on this.

The first weekend in September. You'll stay at the cabin and Pop is going to bunk at my place. I'll take care of the food, drinks and even the clean-up. It's important Aunt Becs.

Now the second thing... the cabin. I don't want you to leave me the cabin in your will... I want you to sell it to me when you're ready. Not Mark and I, just me. With the caveat that you'll come every summer and stay for a minimum of three weeks... like always. And I will never let you tell me to stay away again. EVER!

I love you Aunt Becca, and I'll see in a little over a week

JAKE.

Well, that was some email.

Becca sat there for a few minutes composing herself. She didn't need anyone to see the tears that were rolling down her cheeks.

Damn. She loved the 'little shit'.

He was more her kid than her brothers for a few years when he was growing up. At one point, to piss off his dad most likely, he used to call her mama. He must have been five or six and James was getting married for the third time. Jake didn't warm up to Rhonda in the beginning. And, he never called her mom. He had a mom. She just never saw him. Years later when she finally made an effort, he wasn't that interested. Too much time had passed.

Becca always cherished the time she got with Jake when he was little. It's also when she got to know Justin and when she gave them their nickname, 'JJ'.

When she glanced up, Cain was quietly watching her. He also handed her a Kleenex and took the seat beside her.

"Are you all right baby?" He put his arm around her. She nodded and showed him Jake's email.

"Do you mind if I read it?" She shook her head.

Cain laughed a few times and gave Becca a hug after he finished.

"He seems to be a great young man. Has your sense of humor. I'm really looking forward to meeting him. And the rest of the family, if you still want me to go with you?"

She knew he was asking because of their disagreement from earlier.

She leaned up and gave him a very expressive kiss. After which she whispered into his ear "Yes my love".

Without much forewarning, she changed the subject matter completely.

For some odd reason when she had too much down time, her mind was still trying to wrap its head around that dream/nightmare she experienced.

"Do you remember that weird ass dream I had a few nights back?"

He nodded.

"I think maybe it was brought on by my missing Jakey so much. Just a thought. The minutia of the dream is all but forgotten. It's now just a feeling."

Cain told her that all he really remembered was how terrified, she was when he finally was able to wake her.

They sat quietly for a few minutes, both lost in their own thoughts.

Becca was still reflecting on the odd dream. She somehow felt that in her nocturnal mind, she was a better match for that version of Cain. Still not able to remember why or any specific details, it again was just a feeling. One that she was not willing to share. And yet, for no perceptible reason, it made her a bit sad.

Without any warning, Cain pulled her into a very passionate kiss.

How is he always so perceptive?

"It was just a dream babe. And I think we're a great fit."

Lunch would have to wait since he wished to discuss a few other items regarding their compatibility with her, but it would take privacy and the removal of her clothing.

Definitely a late morning and early afternoon they both enjoyed... a much better outcome than the start of the day.

Joel made them chef's salads, so they didn't need to reheat anything.

'And quite fitting for rabbits'. Becca laughed at her thought. She never told Cain why.

Over lunch she did ask, if he needed anything typed for the affidavits he'd be needing.

He shook his head.

"Are the calls not being productive? Are you worried that your clients won't stay with you?" She was feeling very concerned for her sweet man, whom she loved beyond reason.

"Yes and No. The calls are going a bit slower than I thought they would. A few of my clients that have retired don't want to rock the boat so they'll stay with the company, and I can't blame them for being careful."

"Four of my bigger clients are more than happy to come with me wherever I end up, but I really wanted at least ten for a good showing." He shrugged. But she knew he was more than a little worried.

"I'm going to make a few more calls after lunch and hopefully my luck changes. What are you going to do?" His smile was a little wicked.

"I thought I'd email Jake back and let him know that we are coming to my brother's bash."

He nodded. "After that?"

She shrugged.

He brought her hand to his lips and kissed it ever so gently.

"Come join me in my study after. You can keep me company. And baby, just wear your robe." He put her finger in his mouth and sucked.

Becca felt her whole-body shutter.

"Better yet... go get your robe on now." He released her hand and caressed her right breast since it was the closest.

DAMN! He could arouse her so easily.

She was no longer interested in her salad and moved her chair closer, so he had access to both her breasts... even through her t-shirt they were getting hard. He moved his lips to her earlobe and gave her a stimulating nip. "I think we better take this into our bedroom. Go now." And with that exchange... the afternoon calls would wait.

Cain had Becca on their bed before she had a chance to even think about putting on a robe. He got her pants and panties off in record time and took full advantage of her very ready state.

It didn't happen very often, but he climaxed before her. And of course, being ever diligent with his promise of twelve hundred orgasms he wasn't about to leave her wanting and pulled out the vibrator, called 'the Grey', which they bought several weeks earlier. He then made sure, she had a very satisfying experience with aftershocks.

Once he accomplished that task, he finished removing the rest of her clothing informing her that she wouldn't need any for the rest of the day.

It would seem that he had Becca right where he wanted her.

Cain loved playing with her breasts, and he was driving her crazy with the sensation his lips were inflicting. He also turned the vibrator back on and kept a steady rhythm while, he sucks and teased the girls.

Her moans fueled his assault and right when she was about to have yet another climax he replaced 'the Grey' with her favorite sex toy, and they both had a very powerful release.

She was spent, as was Cain. He wrapped her in his arms, and they drifted off into a well-deserved late afternoon siesta.

Becca loved waking up in Cain's arms. She felt treasured and was trying to remember if she'd ever felt that way before.

That would be a 'No'.

She also noticed that the dildo was lying next to her.

Why yes, that did give her an idea. Thank you for keeping up.

Although she did very much appreciate the fact that Cain felt some bizarre need to make sure she got his arbitrary number of orgasms, she would rather he skipped the sex toys, except of course for her favorite one. Which you all know is attached to him and very effective.

She went into her closet to grab a robe and hide the vibrator.

It would be taking a swim sometime in the near future.

Feeling rather happy with that thought she made her way into their bathroom to take another shower.

Again, never really surprised when he joined her.

He pulled her into his arms and whispered in her ear. "Baby, where is it?" She feigned ignorance to what he could possibly be referring to and got a rather audible slap on her ass. She grinned since it was his mischievous smack... the one that usually aroused her.

Deciding to be a bit wicked herself, she reached down and caressed his penis and reminded him that it was her favorite sex toy and all others failed in comparison so, perhaps he could forget about the one he must have misplaced.

"Why thank you babe, but I would still like for you to return what you've taken. In fact, I'm feeling a bit 'twitchy' about it." His look was stern and evil as he pinned her to the shower wall.

Before she had a chance to speak, he took ownership of her mouth.

Now, have you ever had one of those little occasions of sheer embarrassment during a very intimate moment?

Well of course you have.

Normally it wouldn't have phased Becca in the slightest but at that precise second, she was mortified when her stomach growled.

We're not talking about a little noise but one that seemed to reverberate off the shower walls.

Cain laughing didn't help.

She was out of the shower grabbing a towel and was in her closet in seconds. It was only the second time she ever locked the door.

The first was when she redacted a certain book's contents.

He knocked but got no reply. "Baby, I'm sorry I laughed." It didn't help his cause when he started to laugh again. All he had to do was just think about it and had to walk into his own closet so, he didn't piss her off any more than she currently was.

Joel knocked on the main door to let them know dinner would be ready in ten and got a 'thank you' from Cain.

Back at her closet door. "Come on Becca. Joel has dinner almost ready."

He reframed from saying anything about her obviously being hungry for fear she wouldn't eat.

Food and weight were still a tender subject with her, and it drove him nuts since he loved the way she looked, always had, always would.

He knocked again. "Please come have dinner with me?"

This time the closest door opened, and Becca emerged fully dressed, shoes and socks included. And without giving Cain much of a look handed him the dildo, she stole earlier and headed out of their stateroom.

Cain tossed the toy on the bed and claimed her hand as they headed to the dining room.

Let's clear this up since some of you are disparaging about the use of vibrator and dildo to describe the same object.

Well, you are correct that the two can be separate items and used for different effects. However; in the case of 'the Grey', it is in fact a vibrating dildo. So, let's move on, shall we?

Joel prepared a lovely 'Chicken Marsala' but did inform them that, he Americanized it a tad by adding pasta.

Dinner was a very solemn event since there wasn't much of a conversation between our two lovebirds.

Becca did eat and that pleased Cain. But, how was he going to get her to have a serious conversation about food and body image?

Not a clue. Good Luck! with that.

She was still feeling very self-conscious about her earlier bodily outburst and just wanted to eat and go watch a movie. Or take a walk on deck.

Having enough of the tension, Cain cleared the table, and put the dishes in the sink for Joel to take care of later. He then pulled Becca into his arms and led her to his study.

"You and I are going to clear the air, because this is beyond stupid. So-what if your stomach growled. I will admit the timing was priceless and funnier than hell and if it were me, you would have laughed your ass off. In fact, it wasn't that long ago I let go a pretty loud fart in a very intimate moment and you nearly wet yourself with hysterical laughter." He stroked her cheek and she nodded.

"Baby, you are fit and beautiful and I happen to love every inch of you. So, can we please move on now?"

He was of course right... 'jackass'.

She smiled at him knowing that he wouldn't let her out of his office until her mood improved.

"Good. Now, would you please tell me why you don't like that very effective toy? Your body responds to it quite nicely."

Cain noticed a sadness in her eyes and pulled her back into his arms.

She was looking down as she spoke. "That's all I had to use to relieve my sexual tension for well over a decade. You're better." She hugged him tighter.

He tilted her head up to look him in the eye. "Thank you for telling me. I'm not saying I won't use it again because I love watching you climax, but I will take your feelings into consideration. But baby, you're not alone anymore. And you're not allowed to use it without me, deal?"

She nodded and even blushed.

He gave her a very tender kiss.

"How about, you and I take a walk on the deck this evening?" He was wearing her smile.

She nodded with true enthusiasm that time.

After a nice evening stroll, Becca read another three chapters of Treasure Island that night finishing the tale.

'Great Expectations' was next.

Cain gave her a very lovely thank-you kiss, and they both enjoyed getting their sleep pattern back to normal.

SATURDAY

When Becca woke the next morning, Cain was again sitting next to her, just watching her sleep. "Good Morning."

She smiled and wished him a good morning as well.

"We'll be in San Diego just after lunch. Once we've secured 'SIRA' and Steve and the 'Kid' arrive with the cars, we will all be leaving the yacht for several weeks. And I was thinking you and I could go to your Nevada residence. I'll be able to work from there and finish up my calls and hopefully get more of my clients on my side before we have to go back east. And of course, there is a surprise birthday party you and I have to attend as well." He smiled her smile.

She knew he was waiting for her response. But one little issue was bothering her and had been. Time to put all the cards on the table. Or some at least.

"Okay. Sounds like a good plan. The only thing..." she paused to find the right words. "The property in Nevada is pretty basic, not too many frills. Very homey. Well below your standards I'm afraid."

"Babe, have you been worried about this? No need, I will be happy and content anywhere you are. I don't care, if we stay in a cardboard box." He gave her a very loving kiss.

She really adored him for lying. What a sweet man.

But that also made her realize that Cain didn't always have the yacht, where did he live before?

"I've never asked you this, but you where did you live prior to having 'SIRA'?"

"I had a place in downtown Seattle for several years. Sold it this past spring and began looking for a marina to moor this beast, one that I'd like to call home. After designing and building my girl here… I knew I'd either live aboard or somewhere very close by. However; with either choice, I wanted the climate to be warmer and drier than the Pacific Northwest." He winked and left her to get ready for the day.

After breakfast, Cain went to get some work done, and Becca went to email her nephew.

She also decided to email Mary again to let her know that they'd be there sometime in the next few days and would she please stop by her place and air it out before their arrival.

That also made her realize that she needed to get her best friend a suitable thank you' gift.

Mary had a very impressive magnet collection that took up her entire refrigerator as well as her freezer. They were souvenirs from every place she'd ever been or gifts from friends and family of places they'd travelled. She would be getting eight more from Becca's travels but that wasn't good enough. She'd need to think hard about a special 'bestie' present.

That too reminded her about all the notes she'd kept from Cain. She needed to get that gift going as well.

Come to think of it... she'd need something for her brother's sixtieth. 'A walker maybe or some Depends,' she laughed at the thought.

Time to research a bit and see what's around the Kona Kai Marina. She didn't like shopping, but it would be handy in this instance for something to be close by.

WOW!

Kona Kai Marina has loads of amenities. It's the closest marina to the open ocean in San Diego Bay. Plus, it offers boat owners deep water moorage and no bridges between their marina on Shelter Island and the Bay or Pacific Ocean.

Kona Kai can accommodate thirty-foot vessels all the way up to two-hundred and fifty-foot Mega Yachts and has over five hundred slips.

And, now that they have acquired Kona Kai Resort, they have even more to offer.

'Oh cool. They are only minutes from downtown and walking distance to some of the finest San Diego shopping'.

One problem is solved.

Don't believe everything you read. Just saying.

She imaged Cain was pleased that Kona Kai is a member of the 'California Clean Marina's Program' and has been since 2005. He likes to do his part to protect the environment so, having a marina with the same mantra is a great thing.

Repair facilities are also within walking distance. 'Good for Frank.'

Free Wi-Fi. Again... score!

It's been mentioned on several instances... it's the little things that sometimes bring the most glee.

But what Becca was the most excited to find in her search, was a beach at the resort and anyone staying at the marina had full access. The idea of going swimming just brought a huge smile to her face.

Of course, she would have to let Cain know if she was going since he did tend to have an issue with water.

Much more understandable in light of what he told her.

"What has put that lovely smile on your face baby" Cain chuckled, since he scared the crap out of her. Again.

No huge shocker there.

"You need a damn bell around your neck." Becca gave him a stern look. "But to answer your question, I was reading all about Kona Kai Marina and they have a private beach." That still brought back her smile.

He nodded but didn't look nearly as pleased as she was.

"Cain, I will be careful. Please don't worry about me and ocean swimming. I never go too deep. I've seen 'Jaws' one too many times for that." She took his hand as he came and sat down next to her on the couch.

"I'll try, but more than likely I will still want to be there with you, just to make sure." He kissed her hand.

Not wanting to fight about that subject for what seemed like the hundredth time, she showed him the website she was looking at.

"Becca, go to the map of slips please." She did.

He pointed at the screen. "There, dock 'E' that's where we'll be calling home for the next few months. But what I came out to discuss was the idea of going to Hawaii for the winter? Of course, this will be after our trip to Idaho and the one to New York." He had on her favorite smile.

"You're joking right? Who in their right mind would say no to Hawaii?" She shook her head bewildered by this man.

"Then I can take that as a yes."

She nodded.

He took her face in his hands and gave her a very affectionate kiss.

"Good. And since you're in a 'yes' mood. I'm thinking we should get married on the islands, let's say in January." He was looking right into her eyes, and she was beyond floored by his suggestion.

Flabbergasted might be a better word. Since utterly shocked didn't quite fit the bill.

"What? You're kidding me, right?"

Not quite the response, he was hoping for since he dropped his hands from her face and sat back like she'd actually hit him.

"Oh. You weren't. Cain I'm sorry, I didn't mean to upset you or hurt your feelings. But, it's a little sudden don't you think, to be talking about marriage I mean… hell, I'm not even employed anymore. And your situation in New York isn't resolved. Plus, I've not met your folks and you've not met my family." She was grasping at every proverbial straw she could think of… it was a bit more rambling than intended but, in her defence, she was still stunned by his very strange proposal. In her mind, it came out of nowhere.

"I made my intentions known when I moved this ring to your left hand. So, no I don't think it's all of a sudden. I know, I want you to spend the rest of your life with me. And Rebecca Lynne Curtis has a nice ring to it. Furthermore, you do have a job, working for me. I'm not concerned about New York and meeting family has no bearing on our future." He was holding her left hand and playing with the lovebird ring he'd bought for her in Juneau a month earlier.

"I love you Cain, you know this, and I can promise you that I'll not marry anyone but you. However; in saying all that, I need you to wait for a few weeks and ask me again once this mess in New York is resolved because I do think it matters more than you're letting on and since you're forcing my hand in regards to my family, I would like you to make a trip home to see yours" She leaned in and gave him a quick kiss.

"Your situation with your brother is much different than my circumstances with my mother are and I don't think that should be a factor in our marriage plans. I just stated that our family shouldn't' dictate our future plans together. Did you ever consider that I may not be ready to see her?" He looked lost in thought.

Not willing to back down from the topic... Becca put her foot down. "I don't care if you're ready or not. I would give anything for five more minutes with my mom or my dad for that matter. So, if you really want to marry me... that's the best gift you could ever give me. You making peace with your mom and seeing your dad in person. It's been too long, and they aren't getting any younger."

Fiery redheads… Gotta love em.

Matching her stubborn tone. "Fine, but you're coming with me." And with that he tossed her IPad onto the seat next to her and pulled her into a rather intimate kiss.

He should have thought of that before, then she'd never gotten around to playing the 'mom' card. Just saying.

Damn, what that man can do with just his lips.

Joel's well-placed cough got both Becca's and Cain's attention.

"Sorry to interrupt but I was going to heat up the leftover Chinese food for everyone to have for lunch. If it's okay with you Mr. Cain, I was hoping to feed everyone out of the one galley today, since we're getting close to docking?"

Cain nodded and stood pulling Becca to his side. She was still blushing a bit from being caught, for the umpteenth time.

"Call us when it's ready please, we'll be in the office." He grabbed her IPad as he escorted her out of the living room.

Joel being Joel, he couldn't just reheat their takeout from the night before last. No-No, he had to recreate their lunch to a whole new level.

Under his culinary skills; Szechwan chicken was mixed with Kung Pao shrimp and the remaining Chow Mein to make a spicy noodle dish. He took the leftover rice and made fried rice with the foil-wrapped chicken, Egg Foo Young and beef skewers. And the orange and lemon chicken became one mouth-watering citrus dish. He got kudos from everyone.

Especially from Becca who got a Caesar salad with halibut. Good Man.

Just after the crew ate lunch the captain steered them into San Diego Bay and a short time later, they were at their new digs inside Kona Kai Marina, dock E-slip fourteen.

Everyone was on the upper deck looking around. It was a very pleasant day, sunny with a slight breeze coming off the Pacific Ocean.

Becca was taking in their surroundings. She made note that they were not on the farthest dock, but it was still quite the walk to the parking lot. And a bit longer to the beach she found on their website.

They all seemed in awe of the Mega-Yachts they could see from where they were tied up.

With wide eyes, she was glad she only thought 'Holy Shit those are some huge 'fuckers'. Twice the size of 'SIRA' and then some.'

Cain put his arm around her and whispered. "I know you're thinking the 'f' word." She just shook her head.

Again. FREAK!

"Should I pack today or will tomorrow be soon enough?" She was changing the subject since thinking a word shouldn't matter.

"Tomorrow is fine. The boys just left San Francisco and won't be here until late tonight or early tomorrow. It would seem the repair was a bit more in-depth than originally thought. They'll need a little rest and more than likely we will all leave the day after tomorrow." He kissed her head.

"Would you mind if I went swimming then?" She leaned her head back into his shoulder.

"How about tomorrow? I need to call a few more people and can't go with you right now." He tightened his arms.

She nodded.

Cain thanked her for waiting and headed below deck to get back to work.

Becca figured she might as well get her stuff organized for packing and maybe do a little more web surfing regarding shopping areas for the gifts she needed to find.

Of course, nothing was quite as close as she was led to believe from her earlier search, so walking wasn't the best idea.

Sort of mentioned that.

Options that popped into her head. Walking to the stores and cabbing back seemed like a good idea.

This vast marina had lots of perks, perhaps they offered a shuttle service. No time like the present... she needed to find out.

A quick text to Cain letting him know that she was heading out to explore the marina and would seem him later.

Becca was just coming to the end of the 'A' dock when he replied telling her to have fun, but no swimming.

She smiled and shook her head. He's nothing if not consistent. She was happy to see that the facility office wasn't too far from the ramp she was on. Not a short walk, took just under fifteen minutes.

Kona Kai Marina and Resort are quite substantial.

Their amenities are impressive, but they don't offer a shuttle, much to Becca's disappointment.

The lovely young lady behind the counter, whose nametag read 'Jules' gave her an area map and told her of a few shops that were less than a forty-minute walk away. Doable.

Becca thanked her and headed out to look around the resort debating whether or not to venture out to get the gifts she required.

The idea of shopping wasn't all that exciting, but she did have her list and the rest of the afternoon.

A rather brilliant idea came into her mind!

She texted Joel to see what he was doing at that precise moment in time.

She laughed when he asked her if she was planning on getting him into trouble again.

Their exchange via text…

B: No! I need a shopping buddy and the retail shops are a bit over a mile and a half from here. Want to join me?

J: Okay... give me a minute to put on different shoes. Where are you?

B: Parking lot next to office. See you soon. It's a nice hike from the boat. :)

J: Fuck! Right. See you when I get there.

She really did adore Joel, and she didn't have to watch her language with him. Even better reason to have him come along.

Becca decided she'd better text Cain to let him know she was going to look around a few stores with Joel and she'd see him at dinner.

Covering all of one's bases is a good thing.

She never got a response from Cain, but Joel handed her an envelope when he finally made it down the last ramp and back onto terra firma.

Written on the attached sticky note.

Babe,

Figured you might be getting something for Mary and maybe your brother. Didn't want you to have to worry about finding an ATM. Be safe and have fun.

Always and forever, Your Fiancée, 'C'

She shook her head at the way he finished the note, not that he sent money to her through Joel. And without even looking inside, stuffed it into her purse.

"He caught me, as I was heading down the stairs. You must have called or texted him about me going." Joel had a pointed look and was spot on.

"Yep... didn't want either of us to get into trouble. My bad. Should have waited for you to actually get here before I texted." She shrugged.

She handed him the map and pointed to where they were going. He nodded and they headed out on their retail expedition.

After a few minutes, Joel stopped and looked at Becca.

"When did you get engaged? I mean it's great but sort of sudden, right?" His look wasn't one of shock but close.

"I didn't say 'yes', I told him 'Not yet' and to ask again in a few weeks. Well, you've met the man, so I guess technically we're sort of engaged." Her expression made Joel laugh.

She joined him.

Joel was very easy to like.

The rest of that afternoon was very pleasant, and Becca found a lovely leaded crystal rose that had beautifully etched leaves surrounding the delicate flower. Perfect for her best friend.

She was also thrilled to find a bamboo shirt for her brother, and she even got one for Cain.

Just like the ever-popular sheets, the shirts will also get softer with every wash. She'd found the store in one of her earlier searches.

They took a cab since it was a bit too far to walk, especially after finding out the shopping area was a little over two miles from the marina.

Joel fell in love with the store and after Becca's assurance regarding the quality of the sheets he purchased a set for his and Steve's place back in Washington.

Mary had given Becca a set for Christmas and after only two days she bought another set online. Huge fan.

Must you ask... no, she didn't use Cain's money. That's why God created credit cards. I am surprised you had to go there.

She didn't find a photo shop and would still need to find a couple cards and wrapping paper at some point but for the most part. A very successful outing.

They decided to take another cab back to the marina. Joel's feet were hurting, and truth be told, so were Becca's since she was wearing sandals instead of tennis shoes.

Plus, leaded crystal gets heavy... quick.

Back to Kona Kai just after six with purchases in hand, they headed down to the first security gate.

Locked!

"FUCK!"

They actually said it in unison.

When they came down the docks earlier that afternoon all the gateways were open but it would seem that after five, they are locked, and you need a code to get through.

She called Cain.

After he was done laughing, since he had sort of forgotten about that as well, he went and found the security codes to give them access to the rest of the docks and return to the yacht.

Long fucking walk. Especially with parcels to tote.

Becca wasn't all that surprised to see Cain waiting for them. He pulled her into his arms and gave her a nice hello kiss and offered to carry her packages. She didn't mind that one bit.

He also handed Joel a piece of paper and told him to let Steve know what the codes were so he and the

'Kid' could get on board later that night. Technically, early the next morning. They were expected around two.

"Joel, why don't we just barbeque tonight if you have anything to throw on the grill. Feed everyone on the back deck. Something simple will be perfect." He smiled at his chef.

"Thank you, Mr. Cain, that sounds great. I'll get things going. Should have dinner ready by seven-thirty." He smiled at his employer as he veered off towards the crew quarters.

Becca who was now one step up from Cain, turned and gave her man a very loving kiss letting him know how much she appreciated him. She liked having his face even with hers, 'easy access' as he always says.

Once in the main salon, they both headed to their room. He deposited her bags on the bed.

"Baby, what is so heavy in that one bag. I can't believe you carried that all the way back here." He flexed his hand.

'Wimp'.

"Joel called a cab for the return trip which I'm grateful for since the walk back to 'SIRA' was long enough after our earlier jaunt." She smiled.

She also informed him that the heavy item was the gift she found for Mary. A leaded crystal rose.

That reminded her, she pulled his envelope out of her purse and handed it back to him.

He instantly noticed it was unopened and handed it back.

She shook her head.

"Becca just take it, please." He smiled but it didn't reach his eyes.

"I'll make you a deal. I'll keep the note and you keep the envelope and its contents." She actually smirked at him.

"How about I just put you over my knee for being incredibly stubborn and a bit frustrating." His smirk had an evil component.

Suddenly, feeling very tired of having this same argument again and again. Becca took the damn money back and shoved it into her purse with a bit of force.

Cain raised his eyebrow at her.

'Get the fuck over it' was her only thought to his look.

She now just wanted to take a bath, alone.

He had managed to put her in a very grumpy mood by being a pompous ass and her feet were still hurting.

Becca grabbed the bag with the shirts and pulled out the midnight teal polo that was destined to be his, throwing the bag back on the bed.

"Here, I got this for you." She handed him the article of clothing rather abruptly and without really caring what he thought turned and headed to the bathroom. She informed him, as she shut the door that she'd be taking a bath and would see him in a half hour.

Hell yes, she locked the door.

Becca had just started the waterfall when he knocked and asked to please come in.

No real surprise there, but she didn't want to deal with him and she sure as hell didn't have any desire to have sex.

Mentioned she was grumpy.

She poured the lavender and vanilla bath oil in the tub and placed it back in the cabinet.

Maybe ignoring his request would make him go away.

You really have to laughing at this point... like that was even a remote possibility.

The louder knock made her jump. "Jeez Cain. I'll be out after my fucking bath." She realized what she said a tad late.

'Aw Crap!'

Perhaps having free reign with her language around Joel is not the best thing since it put her guard down. Well, that and being tired and overly annoyed.

Still... she knew that was one button, she didn't want to keep pushing.

'Fuck!' she had to smile since thinking it was her only outlet.

My thoughts... she already let the 'f' word out the box. She should just feel free to say it a half dozen more times. But then again, I'm quite the button pusher myself.

You may have noticed.

No knock came. No stern voice from behind the door. That's either a really bad sign or... nope just bad.

She was now contemplating living in the bathroom until her car arrived.

'Becs, your good gestures go to shit at every turn. Thinking you should quit while you're behind and stop being nice to anyone'. She was still good at self-chastising.

She climbed into the now uninviting tub in a much worse mood.

She'd managed to get two nice blisters on her feet, and now her back was tied up in knots.

Once she actually started to relax, the water felt wonderful. Still, it's hard to enjoy the soak with Cain being angry at her, yet again.

'Why the fuck does he want to marry me, all I seem to do is piss him off. Maybe I am too old for this relationship crap. But I'd miss him like crazy.' As thoughts go... that one blew chunks.

Baths give you way too much time to think.

And with that she hit the drain button before she even got out. She used the hand-held wand to rinse the oils off herself and to rinse out the tub.

Her grumpy attitude from earlier was now just a sadness.

She found a couple band-aids and doctored her feet before opening the door wrapped in a towel.

He was sitting on the bed wearing his new shirt and a pair of dockers.

Damn! He looked gorgeous and sexy as hell. Totally the right color and fit.

"Better?" He was wearing her smile.

She shook her head.

In two strides he had her wrapped in his arms.

She loved his hugs; they gave her such comfort. She loved everything about him. Even his fucking 'twitch'. And the new shirt was very soft and luxurious.

"Baby, would it be okay if we start your arrival from shopping over." She nodded in his chest.

His chuckle reverberated throughout her body.

Her mood improved instantly.

Once seated on their bed, Cain had Becca on his lap and was looking at her feet.

"What shoes caused these?" His caress tickled and she pulled her foot out of his reach.

His look was evil and he slowly captured her foot and moved his fingers along the instep making her squirm.

"Cain, please stop. It was my older sandals." She was laughing as she spoke.

He let her foot go so his hands were able to stroke her back and release the towel she had wrapped around herself.

"You have two choices babe, make-up sex or dinner." He started to kiss her neck and his hands moved from her back to her front.

He was clearly letting her know what his choice was.

Here's the issue. She walked quite a distance and is moody. Very clear signs she needs to eat. So, the smart choice would be dinner.

Oh, for the love of God, of course they had sex... you were doing so well until now.

Joel put dinner in the oven and left them a note with reheating instructions.

They both wore robes as they sat down to finally eat their late supper.

Becca finished well before Cain which only happened on the rarest of occasions.

"I should have realized you needed food. You never get that snappy at me. Especially over something as trivial as a little cash." He shook his head.

"Sorry." She liked their make-up sex so she wasn't totally sincere.

"You know I could still get 'twitchy' on your ass." He raised his eyebrow.

Damn that look is sexy.

He smiled when she shrugged at him.

She got up with her empty plate and headed into the galley. After rinsing it off, she put it in the dishwasher since Joel had retired for the evening.

She was also thinking, she might want to play nice with her man, after all he let her 'f' bomb slide, again.

"Would you like me to get you a bowl of ice cream for dessert?" She gave him her most loving look.

He brought in his plate and put it in the sink.

"What flavors are left?" He had a very interested look on his face.

Becca opened the freezer and told him of the two choices that remained. 'White chocolate with raspberries or Pralines and Cream'.

Since the first one had maybe two good scoops left, Cain opted to finish it off.

She couldn't help but tease him a little.

"Bowl or would you like to finish it out of the container?" she smirked.

"How about I eat it off you, feisty woman?"

Leave it to him to give it a sexual component.

She got him a bowl.

Feeling very domestic all of a sudden, she threw away the now empty container in the trash, rinsed his plate, and put it in the dishwasher grabbed a cloth and wiped down the table.

Cain sat at the galley counter watching while eating his sweet treat.

Once Becca was back at the sink rinsing off the dish cloth he came around and pinned her. He held the spoon to her lips telling her to take a taste. She shook her head.

"Two choices baby. Ice cream or spanking? You choose." He dipped the spoon back into the bowl and got a nice dollop and held it to her now open lips.

It was very tasty, but she hated to eat anything with sugar.

After years of being Diabetic it felt so against the rules.

He hadn't moved so; she was still pinned when he put a second spoonful to her lips.

She took the second bite without any fuss, and he gave her a very nice kiss.

He rinsed the bowl and spoon and put them into the dishwasher himself but didn't let her leave the galley.

He turned back to his future wife and pulled the sash on her robe, so it opened. "Now, that's what I call a proper dessert." His hands pulled her close and his lips started with her earlobes while his hands were much lower. "I'm about to take you right here or would you prefer our room?"

He had her body so alive she didn't care at that point, but thought it best if they moved away from Joel's prep station.

"Room please" and bit down on his earlobe.

His hand made contact with her backside and they moved into a more private setting to continue their physical activities.

SUNDAY

"Becca, where did you find that amazing shirt you gave me? It's the softest I've ever had against my skin."

Cain had her wrapped in his arms as they enjoyed a lazy morning in bed.

It was all of six.

"I found it at the Bamboo store, 'Cariloha'. I have their sheets and knew they had clothing, so that's what I wanted to get James for his birthday and once there, I had to get you one as well." She was quite pleased with herself.

"Do they not have women's clothing?" He gave her a curious look, she just nodded.

"Then why, pray tell, didn't you get something for yourself?" He gave her a soft kiss on the lips.

"Because I didn't need anything." She gave him a quick kiss back and moved like she was getting up.

Pulling her back and trapping her in his embrace. "Where do you think you're going? We're not done talking." His hands took hold of the hem of her nightgown and very easily displaced it on the floor.

He started giving her sweet kisses down her neck while his fingers entertained her breasts. "Baby, I love our mornings in bed. And was thinking now that your car is here, I think you and I should go back and find you something from that bamboo store after we have breakfast." He gave her a very passionate kiss not waiting for a reply.

Again, moans don't count.

Seduced by her man on any morning is a treasured event.

Her body was finally climbing down from the amazing heights of pleasure he gave her that morning. And she found words.

Trust me, they had been eluding her for the past half hour or so.

"My love, I don't need any more clothing but appreciate the gesture." She had her head on his shoulder and was playing with his chest hair relishing being loved.

"Two choices my girl, shopping or spanking? You choose." He was patting her bare ass. And it didn't feel sensual.

'Fuck' was her first thought. The second was, 'How long is he going to use this, choice shit?' She unhappily took shopping as her choice.

His hand came down pretty hard and made a hell of a whacking sound on her butt.

"Ouch!"

"Stop thinking it." His voice was stern. "Up."

When she looked into the mirror before stepping into the shower, she could see a very pink handprint on her backside. 'Damn that man!'

Becca was drinking her second cup of coffee waiting for Cain to return from his study.

Joel was making them omelettes and was using some of the spicy cheese curds he'd picked up just a couple of days prior. Pepper Jack Habanero was going in hers only... Cain's a bit of a wuss, a little hot sauce on occasion to enhance the flavor of scrambled eggs but not too much. He got plain ole cheddar cheese.

She did try to convince Joel to put some of her cheese curds in both, but was informed that he actually liked his job.

"I'm surrounded by wusses." She smirked.

Cain's abrupt return startled her as well as his chef.

Whispering so only Becca could hear. "How sore do you want that pretty little ass of yours? Now please bring up that bamboo store's website." He winked so; she knew he was messing with her.

Joel handed him another cup of coffee while Becca brought up 'Cariloha' for him.

He thanked her as he went through all the women's clothing. When finished he seemed a tad disappointed.

He shut down the laptop as Joel served breakfast.

"What were you hoping to find?" She noticed his good mood had turned.

"Dresses." And then shook his head.

"Take a bite of my omelette and I'll tell you a secret." She had a wicked look. And knew it was quite spicy. Something she enjoyed but he really didn't. Paybacks for his 'twitchy' issues.

Never liking to back down, Cain took the proffered forkful of egg, cheese and mushroom.

His complexion changed to a lovely shade of red as he chewed and swallowed.

It might not have helped that Becca added some extra hot sauce before his bite. Oops.

Joel handed him a glass of milk which he drank in two gulps.

Becca really tried not to laugh, but the look he gave her was quite a sight.

"How in the hell do you eat that spicy shit? It's still burning my mouth." He was drinking another glass of milk a bit slower now.

Becca continued to eat without showing any duress with the heat content of her meal.

Cain just shook his head asking. "Secret?"

Becca let him know that Bamboo dresses are available at several stores, just not that one. Online might be the best option if she were in the market for one but since she wasn't, it seemed irrelevant.

She handed Joel her empty plate and thanked him for a wonderful breakfast. Kissed Cain on the cheek and went to brush her teeth.

Like always, their room was made up to perfection. Stella was a force when it came to cleaning.

She was just spitting and rinsing when Cain reappeared in the bathroom door.

"I've ordered you four dresses to be delivered to the Nevada property but now we need to get you some new sandals. Ones that won't cause blisters." He picked up his toothbrush, and she moved out of his way.

"I don't need new sandals or new dresses for that matter. I want to go swimming today. And there is packing to get done as well."

She didn't want to shop. She shopped yesterday.

He finished brushing and pulled her into a very minty kiss.

"Swimming after shopping and packing will take like thirty minutes." He escorted her out of their stateroom and down to the dock for the long trek to the car.

"You weren't kidding. That is quite the hike to the parking lot." She just nodded since she'd already done it twice the day before.

"Cain, can I ask you something and I really want your honest opinion." She waited for his reply.

"Okay." He sounded almost hesitant. And she rethought her question in her head for a few seconds.

Deep breath, "Do you think I can actually make you happy for the next twenty years? I mean I tend to push your buttons a bit and then there is the water issue. And I really need you to stow that damn twitch of yours? I'm thinking maybe we're just too different."

She knew they loved each other but was that enough.

He didn't miss a beat before answering.

"Becca, I have no doubt that we'll make each other happy for the rest of our lives. Which I hope will be at least forty years. And I think we push each other's buttons. Regarding the water issue, I will always be concerned but as long as I can be with you, I think I can keep it in check. And different is a good thing. Not only do I love every inch of you, body and mind... you make me laugh. I can stow the twitch... not the playful one though." He winked. "Do you see yourself happy with me?" He wrapped her in his arms.

"Yes, I do. In fact, when I think of anything in the future, it's the two of us. Always." She smiled into his chest.

"Good. Now can I ask you something?"

She nodded, loving his arms around her.

"Why did you wait until we were in a parking lot to ask me?" He pulled her chin up so, he could look in her eyes.

"It's a long walk. I sort of formed the questions as we made our way here." She grinned.

"This has been bugging you since last night?" She nodded.

"I wish you'd have talked to me about it then but since I have the same issue about overthinking from time to time. I get it. We're good babe. Always."

She gave him a very passionate kiss.

"Well, part of me wants to take you back to the yacht and push some of your buttons for the rest of the day but since we've made it this far, let's go find you some shoes. And as promised, we have a swim date later."

He gave her another very nice kiss and wrapped his arm around her waist as they walked to where Steve told him the Enclave was parked.

What a great Sunday this was turning out to be. A perfect day with the love of her life. Sheer Bliss.

Except for the shopping part.

They ended up at 'For Bare Feet', 'Bait' and 'Blends'. Cain is nothing if not thorough when it comes to shoe shopping.

Becca was now the proud owner of four new pairs of sandals. Three more than she felt she needed, but there was no arguing with him.

Yes of course, she tried. Seriously, do you need a time out?

Near one of the shoe stores was 'Jai Tunics' and she ended up with two new dresses as well. They were lovely but again, she didn't really need them. Plus, he had already ordered four earlier that morning.

You really don't need to ask if he let her buy any of them... do you?

Why yes, I did roll my eyes. And if you're curious, I can drop the 'f' bomb anytime I wish.

Mistress of my own universe.

Now focus.

"Cain, can we please be done shopping unless you'd like something for yourself?" She tried not to look exasperated. "I like buying you clothes and am looking forward to you wearing every one of the new dresses." His look was very sensuous.

"What happened to my other dress? You know the one that disappeared on Monday." She'd asked him several times, and he evaded the question each time.

"I sort of got carried away and tore it off you in the entertainment room. You didn't notice so I just threw it away." He shrugged

Becca was feeling very flush all of a sudden. 'Caveman'.

Well Damn!

He leaned in and whispered, "you have two choices... bed or swimming?" He kissed her earlobe which sent shivers down her whole body.

They were back at the car when she told him her choice.

"Cain, can I ask you question?" He had been quiet since she chose swimming.

"No." He was sulking.

"So, you're mad at me because you broke your promise? Tad childish don't you think?" She was smirking.

Button pusher.

"I don't see it as a broken promise. It was only going to be delayed." He looked more disappointed than angry.

'I am too fucking old for this shit' She shook her head and sighed.

"Thinking it."

"Bite me."

"I had every intension of doing just that, but you chose swimming." He winked.

Becca couldn't help but laugh.

Mood lightened.

Well Played Mr. Curtis.

Back at the marina they set out to walk back to the yacht.

"So baby, what was the question you wanted to ask me?" He gave her hand a squeeze.

"It's really none of my business but I wondered how you saved such a huge amount of money to afford to build 'SIRA'?"

"I had a good base to start off with. My grandfather left both Frank and I five million dollars in a trust. My dad gave me my brother's money, much to the dismay of my mother, with the stipulation that I couldn't touch it before my thirtieth birthday. Dad also made the caveat, that I had to save at least half the amount of the funds before spending a dime. It was a great incentive, and I was very determined. Plus, I got lucky with some very aggressive investments.

It wasn't until I was in my mid-thirties that I even started to create the blueprints for her." He was pointing to his yacht.

"Frank designed the engine room from the ground up and paid for twenty-five percent of the cost to build her and that's why I put him as co-owner. If you were wondering." He was wearing her smile.

"I'll eventually buy him out with interest, and he knows that, but in the meantime it's a good investment for him."

She nodded

Once back in their stateroom Becca set to hang up her new dresses and get the new sandals on the shoe rack. Her old ones were gone. Not a huge shocker, she figured after they caused the blisters, Cain would kill them. Or throw them away. Either way they would never be seen again.

When she turned around, her handsome and very stealthy man was standing at the closet door with his swim trucks on.

Sexy!

Suddenly she wasn't all that interested in taking that long ass stroll to the beach.

She kicked off her tennis shoes, reached down and removed each sock and then ever so slowly started to unbutton her shirt. Not taking the garment off but letting it open to reveal her lacey bra, she undid the first button on her jeans.

He pounced.

Nope, they never made it swimming.

Becca wore one of the new dresses to dinner, it was cut deep in the front and very sheer and wispy. She was happy it had a built-in bra so, the girls stayed in place. Still, it wasn't really her style, but Cain seemed to approve and even Joel told her it was very becoming.

She blushed at the compliment but loved them all the same.

While they were eating, Becca mentioned about packing and Cain let her know that she would have to do it later. His hand proceeded in traveling up her leg giving her a chill in all the right places.

"Oh baby, thank you for not wearing panties. Scoot forward now." He gave her a wicked grin, as she moaned, and food and packing were replaced by a different hunger.

Damn! What that man could do with just his fingers.

It was well into the evening when she finally got to pack.

She needed an extra bag, which she found in Cain's closet since her wardrobe had been increased by the ever stubborn and overly generous man who was currently asleep.

She would get her toiletries in the morning after a shower.

He still hadn't told her what time they would be leaving.

She'd miss the staff but was looking forward to having Cain all to herself.

Feeling like she accomplished her goal, she took-off her robe and climbed back into bed.

Always sensing her near, Cain reached out and wrapped her in his arms, and they both drifted off to sleep.

MONDAY

"Good Morning Babe. Are you ready to head out for Nevada?" He was showered, dressed and smiling down at her.

When she took stock of their room. Four bags were sitting by the door.

She turned to see how late she actually slept. The clock read six.

'Jeez, in a hurry Cain?' She needed coffee.

"Up and at 'em sleepy head. Joel is making breakfast for everyone. I want to get on the road before eight." He gave her a nice smack on the ass and left their stateroom.

Well, that was one mystery solved. She now knew when they were leaving to venture north eastward.

It was just under nine hours but with stops for fuel and most likely lunch, she figured it would take them close to ten and a half hours for the drive to Ely.

Part of her was tempted to go back to sleep for another hour but her tingling backside told her to get the fuck up.

Not sure what analogy one can draw from that; but, always listen to your butt, especially if its stinging.

Once showered, blow-dried and dressed Becca packed up all her bathroom items in the small case designed for such a purpose. Her toothbrush would be last since she would need it after she ate.

She also made sure to grab her power cords, all of Cain's notes that she'd saved and her IPad. Her phone was already safely in her purse.

Now to go and get coffee and lots of it.

The only reason to ever get up in the morning, mostly.

She was the last to arrive, again. Even the 'Kid' was looking bright-eyed and bushy-tailed. 'Fuck'.

She hated being last... everyone looked up from their breakfast to acknowledge her arrival.

She did the one 'Morning' to all who greeted her.

The only thing that saved her was Joel, who handed her a cup of coffee. 'Thank God, caffeine'.

She was finishing her first cup, when he handed her an English muffin with bacon, cheese and egg stuffed inside. She thanked him and asked for a second cup of coffee, before she started to dissect her morning meal.

Cain's disapproving look wasn't enough to make her eat the bread.

She was really happy he couldn't read her mind, since she was thinking a few very unkind things towards this man, she loved but at that moment in time, she just wanted to kick him in the shin.

Joel broke the tension by giving her a third cup of coffee and removed the offensive muffin.

Becca gave him a huge grin and thanked him for cooking.

"So, who is going where? Do we need to give anyone a lift?" She asked a general question to the whole group.

Frank was the one who filled her in.

"Joel, Steve and I will be heading home to Seattle. Kevin needs to fly back to Tucson to start his junior year at the University of Arizona. Stella and Larry will be heading back home to Phoenix and from what I've gathered, the two of you are going to Nevada." He gave her a wink.

She nodded. Frank was usually very concise and to the point.

Becca went to brush her teeth and pack up her toothbrush and met Cain as she came out of the bathroom.

"Ready when you are." And gave him a quick kiss.

He seemed quite pleased that they were twenty-five minutes ahead of schedule.

He pulled her into one of his wonderful bear hugs.

She could live in those arms forever.

At that moment she knew they would indeed be married on the islands in January, and she had no doubt in her mind that he'd make her happy for the rest of her life.

She only hoped she could do the same for him.

"Becca, what are you thinking about at this very moment?" He pulled away only slightly to look at her face.

"Just thinking how I could live in these arms forever and ever." She nestled back into his chest.

His arms tightened around her.

"And that you shall my sweet girl and that you shall" He kissed the top of her head.

What a lovely intimate moment... interrupted by a rather loud knock on the door.

Hell, they both jumped.

The 'kid' asked if he could grab their bags from the other side of the door and got an affirmative response from Cain.

Becca couldn't help but chuckle and grabbed her smaller bag and purse to make the trek to the car.

She made one look back at their stateroom.

They both would miss 'SIRA' but hoped to be back in six to eight weeks before they left to spend a month or two on the Hawaiian Islands.

They each said their goodbyes to the staff and friends. Becca gave hugs to everyone and was surprised that Cain just shook hands, even with Stella.

For such a passionate man, his formal demeanor with these amazing individuals seemed wrong.

They met Kevin on the dock, and he handed Becca her keys letting them both know that their luggage was all packed and the SUV relocked.

He got a hug and a handshake.

As they continued their long stroll to the parking lot, Cain asked if he might drive.

Like that was ever in question.

She handed him the keys and he retook her hand.

"You've been very quiet on our walk. May I ask what's on your mind?" He brought her hand to his lips.

"You didn't hug anyone goodbye. Not even Frank. I wondered why." She wasn't criticizing, just merely curious.

"I guess I didn't even think about it. I don't often hug Frank." He gave her a smirk.

Becca couldn't help but laugh. Men!

Finally, at the parking lot. She waited for Cain to open her door. He had told her on several occasions that he liked the old fashion gesture. Made him feel gallant.

She just liked the kiss he gave her, each and every time.

Cain took her smaller bag and put it on the back seat before coming around and getting in the driver's side.

"There is a cooler right behind us if you're needing water or anything." And pointed.

"Okay, thanks." She was really wondering where it came from but figured her ever-efficient man made it happen.

"Since you're wondering, Joel provided the cooler and its contents. There is water, fruit, cheese and even a protein shake." He grinned as he pulled out of the parking lot and headed for highway 5.

She nodded. 'Kreskin'.

Becca loved having her iPod back. She'd been missing her music, and since Cain was driving, she took full control of the tunes.

She also got them each a water from the cooler. Being the ever-attentive co-pilot.

"It's a long drive baby, tell me about Ely." He released her hand to turn the music down a bit.

"You want the history, or the chamber of commerce take?" She gave him her best 'I'm totally fucking with you look'.

He grabbed her knee and gave it a firm squeeze.

He made his point, and she gave him a detailed dialogue on the town of Ely, Nevada.

"Ely was founded in White Pine County as a gold camp in 1878 by a Vermont prospector named 'Long'. Lots of theory's where the name originated from. Some think it's because this 'Long' fellow was from Ely, Vermont. Others say it was named for the New York representative that sent him on the scouting expedition. Still others think it was from the gentleman who funded him, and the last guess is that an Illinois native named John Ely actually named it. I don't think anyone will ever be sure which story is accurate."

"The town itself grew not only because of the mine, but also because it was a stagecoach station along the Pony Express and Central Overland Route.

The first mining operation started in the early 1900's when copper was discovered. Kennecott is still the biggest mining operation in the town. I noticed that the same company had a gold mind operation just outside Juneau, Alaska. They get around." She paused.

Cain nodded.

"Anyway, Ely really relies on tourism these days and is home to the Northern Nevada Railway Museum. The railroad museum features the Ghost Train of Old Ely, a working steam engine that travels the historic tracks from Ely to the Robinson mining district as a passenger train. It's a ninety-minute ride if you're interested in going and every Friday night during the summer, they offer the 'Great Basin Star Train' It's really wonderful. I've only done it once but that's an option as well, if they are not sold out. Which happens every year." She stopped to gauge his interest.

He didn't seem to be listening anymore, so she ended her history lesson.

Becca moved to turn the music back up and Cain grabbed her hand.

"Baby, why did you stop talking? Ely sounds fascinating." He kissed her hand.

"You weren't listening." She was sure he was lost in his own thoughts while she was speaking.

"I was too listening." He sounded quite offended.

He went on to explain. "When you mentioned the train, it reminded me of my brother. He had a train set when we were kids. I was not allowed to touch it. He gave me my first black eye when I did." He was chuckling at the memory.

"Please continue," he reclaimed her hand and gave it a gentle squeeze.

"Okay. Well, Ely sits on the Eastern edge of Highway6 which is called 'Nevada's Loneliest Highway'. The town is just under sixty-five hundred feet above sea level in elevation and has just over four thousand residents. It's a very quaint town with a kind of rural bohemian feel. There are over twenty murals and sculptures along the main street through town that depict its history. We average under ten inches of rain a year, but on average we have over six months of freezing temperatures at night. Very quick growing season, less than three months. But since I haven't got a green thumb, it doesn't affect me. Mary on the other hand gets downright vicious if her tomatoes get frozen." She smiled.

"I am looking forward to meeting your best friend. She sounds like quite the lady. How did you meet and what made you choose Ely as your home?"

They were now on Highway 215 heading towards the I-15 which would take them through Las Vegas.

"I was working with Nevada tourism, selling different magazines that are available around the state. You know the ones that tourists pick up to find out all about the town they're visiting, sights to see and things to do." She smiled since she'd picked up several on their Alaska trip.

He also smiled and nodded since she read to him several times out of each one.

"Anyway, that's one reason I can recite the history of Ely so easily. The job I had with them required a lot of travel so, every three to four weeks I was in Vegas. They had several publications, and the most money to spend so, it was always a lucrative place to sell." She paused for a sip of water.

"Mary worked for one of the huge timeshares there and my company owned one of the units. When it wasn't in use by senior staff or special guests, I got to stay there. I met Mary one day in the lobby, and we became friends almost immediately. She's easy to like. Very outgoing, beautiful inside and out and incredibly blunt. I think she's rubbed off on me after a year or ten." Becca smiled at that.

Cain squeezed her hand again.

"Just a bit baby." He was pulling off at Barstow.

'Pit Stop! Yes!'

They'd been driving just over two and a half hours and they both needed a restroom and a stretch.

Cain pulled into the 'Starbucks'. Not a huge shocker since he was the only person who loved coffee as much or more than Becca.

The line unfortunately was out the door.

"So, how bad do you want coffee?" She gave him a questioning grin.

His look told her to get her ass in line.

She had finally made it into the actual building when he came to take her spot so, she could go take her turn using their facilities.

"How are they?" She was almost afraid to ask.

"Let's put it this way, I'm glad I get to stand up." He had the decency to look apologetic.

'Fuck!'

Still shouldn't count if she thinks it. And headed to the bathroom.

His raised eyebrows told her different.

'Lighten up!'

Her angelic smile didn't fool him one bit.

By the time she was back, he had just ordered and asked what took her so long.

"There was a line there too." She shrugged.

He nodded.

"I ordered you a large, iced coffee with room for cream." She smiled since that is her go to drink when at 'Starbucks'.

One they didn't mess up.

Cain got his usual Macchiato with an extra shot and added a couple of cookies to his order. He asked Becca if she'd like to drive into Vegas.

Once there, she'd get to go to 'Dutch Bros' her all-time favorite coffee stop. She'd missed them.

"Wow, drive my car. What a concept." She smirked.

While doctoring her coffee he leaned down and whispered that her sarcasm made him feel 'twitchy'.

Becca decided to just ignore that statement and moved on to a totally new topic since he'd promised to stow the twitch, and she knew it was just an idle threat. Still… best not push it.

"You want to grab sushi for lunch once we're in Las Vegas?"

He kissed her cheek, handed her the keys and gave her an affirmative nod.

Once back in the car Becca couldn't help but feel like she was sitting in the backseat.

'Jeez he has long legs,' and proceeded to move the seat up so she could actually reach the gas and brake.

She'd not driven her car in well over a month and a half. It felt strange to be back behind the wheel.

Once safely on the I-15, she knew they were just over two hours away from their next stop, barring any traffic issues.

"Okay, so you left off where you and Mary had just met and liking her bluntness. Was she married? Is she now?" He was making short work of his second cookie.

She couldn't look at him and that sucked but this part of the highway had heavy traffic with eighteen wheelers who seemed to merge at the most inconvenient times, and this required her eyes to remain on the road. That and they never went their posted speed.

Then again, neither did she, so she blew by several trucks as fast as she could before the third lane disappeared.

"I thought the passenger had to entertain the driver? Why don't you regale me with more of your history?"

Worth a shot, right?

"I like hearing your voice and you weren't finished so, please continue."

She knew he was smiling and serious.

She was thinking about Mary and remembering a less complicated time in her life. Of course, that would have been the most complex time in Mary's life. Funny how they never seemed to be content at the same time. Odd.

"Becca, you're lost in thought. " And he squeezed her hand.

"Sorry. Yes, she was still married when I first met her. He was a real douche named Doug Anderson. It was the first time I witnessed mental abuse up close. He controlled the finances, and she never had more than twenty dollars at any given time. When she told me that he checked her credit card activity every day, I was livid. I hated him from the start and the way her treated her, but it wasn't my business to interfere. Well, not then it wasn't. I sort of made myself a promise to help free her of whatever hold he seemed to have on her. If she asked. Maybe even if she didn't" She smiled and took a drink of her coffee.

"Oh babe, do go on. This is getting very interesting." He gave her hand another squeeze before she put it back on the steering wheel due again to heavy traffic.

"It took over a year for her to see that there was a better life waiting for her. It started with asking the company she worked for to give any bonuses she had coming by check instead of direct deposit. Mary was so scared Doug would find out and hurt me, but I wasn't concerned. He wasn't physical and most bullies are cowards. Anyway, when she started getting the extra checks, she would sign them over to me and I put them into a money market account in my name only. She would tell the 'scumbag' that sales were down, and competition was at an all-time high when he asked about the drop in her income. He bought it for quite a while."

She stopped talking for a couple of minutes since the heavy traffic was getting more congested which required her full attention.

"That took a lot of trust on her part, and it could have put you in danger babe. Bullies do lash out sometimes." He brought her hand to his lips.

Becca could tell by his tone that this part of the story wasn't making him very happy.

'Tough shit! You do what you have to for friends and family.' She would have moved mountains to free Mary from that prick. That is; after all, what best friends are for.

The highway traffic opened back up and her tension diminished.

"Baby I have to ask since you helped her out of her bad marriage." He didn't get to complete his question before her response. Truth be told she'd been expecting it.

"Yeah, yeah... I know. I'm a huge hypocrite but my situation was years later, and I guess when you live it, you don't always see what's right in front of your face. It gave me great insight into what she went through or at least I was much more sympathetic to her circumstances. And if you're wondering why she didn't help me... simple really... I was so much better at keeping my feelings to myself. Until I wasn't." She looked over briefly at her lovely man.

"Becca, I think there is something huge that happened and you've kept it to yourself long enough. Will you please tell me? It seems to still cause you pain."

Her response was a mere whisper. "No".

He never let go of her hand for the rest of the drive into Vegas, but let her turn the music back up as they sat in quiet reflection for the last thirty minutes.

Once in the 'Neon Capital of the World', she needed both hands to maneuver through all the idiots on the road.

Cain also gave her a pass on using the word 'fuck' when a Ford F-150 pulled in front of her and slammed on its brakes.

IQ tests should be given along with driving tests…that should clean up the roads a bit. Maybe.

Becca had driven around Vegas for over eleven years doing sales and recalled hating it then, it was worse now.

With no preamble. "How hungry are you? There is an all you can eat place that is amazing but not exactly cheap called, 'Biwon Korean BBQ and Sushi' or one that serves individual rolls called 'Sushi Fever'."

"Second one, I think. Don't you?" She nodded.

Once off the freeway and on surface streets, she made her way down Sahara to their lunch destination. A little out of the way but one of her favorite spots. She would have been fine with either choice since both were good in their own right.

Once parked she happily gave Cain back the keys since he would take over driving after they ate.

He pulled her into a huge hug, and she melted into those wonderful arms.

"Baby, I know it's around four hours to Ely, but would it be okay with you if we got a hotel here for the night?" He gave her a very nice kiss.

During lunch he made a reservation at the Bellagio, making sure their room overlooked the fountains below.

Even on a Monday, not the least expensive place to stay on the strip, but it has an amazing view.

She was still a little confused why they needed a room since it was only twenty minutes to two in the afternoon. They could easily make Ely before nightfall.

"Becca are you wondering why I booked us a room?"

Damn he is perceptive.

She nodded.

He waited for the waitress to put down the rolls they ordered.

Cain had way too much fun with the names. He tried to get Becca to order the 'Screaming Orgasm' or 'Sex on the Beach', but she refused.

He did however get the blush he was after.

They ended up with a 'Crunch Roll', a 'Monica Roll, a 'Grand Canyon Roll' and a hand roll called 'The Kamikaze'. He also ordered them 'Plum Sake' to share.

They ate for a couple minutes before he finally answered her unasked question.

"Baby, I just want to get you into bed." And he winked at her.

Well yeah... Huge blush.

Becca had tried a couple pieces of the three delicious choices they'd made and was feeling a tad full since she had eaten some apple slices and a piece of cheese a few hours before. She laughed when Cain pretty much inhaled the hand roll. Apparently, it was quite tasty.

She was reminded of her dissected breakfast and ate three more pieces of the 'Monica Roll' since it had the most spice and that seemed to satisfy her dining companion. It was also her favorite roll.

"What's on your mind Becca? You have a very odd expression." He finished off the second roll.

"I lied to you a few weeks back, and I'm feeling guilty about it." She put down her chopsticks.

"Would you like to wait until we're by ourselves in our room?" He pointed to the last five pieces, and she shook her head to both questions.

"You remember when I mentioned that I would never be able to retire and how upset that made you?" He nodded.

"Well, we didn't know each other very well and I knew by then that I was falling in love with you, but I didn't know how you were feeling so, I left out a few details." He raised his eyebrow.

Sort of his tell that she was to continue.

"The tourism company I worked for before I was married and the few years following, set up a nice 401Kfor me and matched my contribution up to a certain percentage each and every year I worked for them. I moved it into a money market account when we parted ways and I've been putting money into it these past several years when I've had extra cash to spare." She was blushing a bit.

"Becca, please don't feel guilty about that. I'm thrilled that you have money to retire, and it wasn't really any of my business and besides that, you've never once asked about my net worth." He reclaimed her hand into his.

"Of course, once we're married, we will have to amend that to our finances." He winked and gave her, her favorite smile.

She'd thought about that since he asked her to tie the knot. 'That discussion could wait for another time.' And she smiled back.

"Now, let's go check in to our hotel."

She got a very 'G' rated kiss since they were still at the restaurant.

Once they stepped in their Bellagio tower room with the incredible view of the 'Strip' as well as the fountain show below, he intensified their kiss, showing his extreme passion and desire for his fiancé.

Becca barely had time to even register the amazing vista, before she found herself on a very comfortable king size bed. Defiantly an 'R' rating from that moment on. Might even have gotten an 'X' at one point.

Damn!

Cain kept her very entertained for the rest of the afternoon into the early evening.

Reality speaking… he wore her the hell out.

She woke just as the sun was starting its descent and the music was letting her know that the fountain show was about to start, again. She got up with the hopes of not disturbing her adoring man and went and stood at the window looking down at the water show. The lights of the strip were in full swing. 'What a glorious view.'

Paris was directly across the street. The Aria was to the right with Caesar's Place to the left. Quite lovely indeed.

Becca leaned back into Cain when he came and stood behind her resting her head on his shoulder. "Thank you for today my love."

His arms wrapped around her naked body. "You don't need to thank me for something that gave me such pleasure. But you're welcome, and the day is not over baby."

He kissed her neck and moved his hands to their target and got Becca's nipples to harden at his expert touch.

As the music continued... so, did Cain's sensual attack with just those astute lips and traveling fingers.

Her crescendo was perfectly timed with the end of the dancing fountain.

The encore had a perfect accompaniment with her favorite sex toy back on the ever so comfy king size bed.

Damn!

Nope just Damn!

"Becca, wake up baby. I poured us a bath and I want to take you out for a late supper." A quick and well-placed smack on the ass got her attention. Usually arousing but not so much after their marathon of sexcapades.

"I'm not hungry. Why don't you go eat and I'll sleep since you really are trying to kill me with orgasms?" In her sleepy brain, it sounded very reasonable.

The next light slap on her ass let her know that he didn't agree. Her slow pace got a stern warning of carrying her into the bath and dropping her in.

She finally got up.

The spa tub was nice but nothing like the one on the yacht. They were very spoiled.

The garden tub at the Ely house was also nothing close to what Cain was used to. She hoped he'd be okay with her very rustic home. Their home if they really got married.

"What has you lost in thought Becca?" He was just starting to wash her feet and legs.

"Just thinking about the difference in tubs. Miss yours actually" She couldn't help but blush since that might include those well-placed jets.

"Do you now. Jets and all?" His teasing tone made her blush even more.

She splashed him.

GAME ON!

There was now, more water on the floor than in the tub and Becca was suitably drenched from Cain's attack.

She started it!

Still, he did take it to the extreme.

Nope, not at all surprised.

Becca went to step out of the tub without really concentrating on her footing.

Yep, right on her ass.

Oh, come on... you'd laugh too!

Cain couldn't contain his laughter since her expression was beyond priceless, and he could tell that she wasn't injured, just embarrassed and pissed off.

Once back on her feet, she grabbed a bath towel and wrapped it around herself and threw every other towel onto the wet floor ensuring her, still laughing man, didn't get one.

'Paybacks are a bitch.' As he frequently informed her.

Once in the main part of the room she used the same towel to dry her very wet head and got dressed in jeans since that's what she grabbed before they checked in.

"Babe, can I use your towel?" She tossed it at him.

"It's wet." He was holding it at arm's length.

"Huh, really... a towel got wet when used to dry off excess water. Odd." She smirked at him.

She still marvelled and very much enjoyed the view of his gorgeous naked body and that incredible ass.

Woof!

He winked noticing her appreciative look and threw the wet towel on the floor with the rest, he then went into the closet and grabbed one of the robes provided by the hotel.

He also handed Becca one of the dresses he bought her in San Diego just the day before. He also handed her the sandals that lace up her calf.

She was holding the garment but making no effort to put it on. Her look was curious. The shoes were now on the floor.

"While you were sleeping, I went back down to the car to get us some clothes to wear out this evening." He loved to answer her unspoken questions.

She nodded but again wasn't making an effort to redress.

"Babe, I really want to take you out. What's on your mind?" His hand was on her chin tipping it up so he could see her eyes.

"You spend too much money on me." She found herself wrapped in his arms. The robe he had on was very soft and fluffy.

"I don't think I spend nearly enough on you so, be good and go blow dry your hair and get into that lovely dress. Panties are optional, you decide." He gave her a very tender kiss and released her pointing to the bathroom.

She spent the first several minutes mopping up the water with all the towels that were on the floor.

Once she had the minor flood under control Becca went and started to blow dry her hair.

When she looked in the mirror, Cain was watching her from the door. He just smiled and nodded before leaving her in peace.

When she finally came back out, now dressed for dinner in her lovely frock and yes, panties too, she found her handsome man in black slacks, crisp white shirt and a dinner jacket. Damn, he looked hot.

She laced up the sandals that were still on the floor where she dropped them.

"Damn woman, you look beautiful." And he held out his hand for her to take.

"You're quite a handsome sight yourself, my love." He lifted her hand to his lips and gave it a kiss.

"Let's go my girl, we have reservations at 'Lago' for nine-thirty." And with that, he escorted her from their room down to the Italian Restaurant next to the fountains for their evening repast.

She loved that he picked a very casual place to dine. They were dressed more than suitable for the low-key atmosphere.

Their table was right next to the window, and Becca loved being so close to the fountains.

If not for the panes of glass she felt that she could reach out and touch the water.

Again… Amazing!

Cain took his jacket off and put it over the chair across from them and took the seat right next to Becca. She was all smiles and squeezed his hand.

"Thank you." She leaned her head on his shoulder.

"You're welcome, baby. Would you like a glass of wine this evening?" His fingers on her bare back sent shivers everywhere.

"No, but you should have one." He nodded.

When the waiter returned Cain ordered several dishes along with a glass of wine for himself and bottled water with lemon for them both.

"That seems like a lot of food for just the two of us." She'd been so busy looking at the fountains and her handsome man that she hadn't even opened the menu.

"'Lago' is known for their small plates with big bold favors. We'll get to try several Italian dishes without the guilt. So, I will expect you to try everything." His look was full of love with a serious undertone.

"Do you now?" She couldn't help but shake her head since he was giving her his 'don't mess with me about this' look.

Very sexy.

The fountains started and distracted her again.

She apologized to Cain for her diverted attention.

His lips let her know it was all good.

'Shit, when did the drinks come?'

The wine on his lips tasted pretty damn good.

She vowed to herself to be more considerate from that moment on.

They started their meal with butternut puree soup along with an heirloom tomato and mozzarella salad. Both were exceptional.

He wasn't kidding. They were very small plates offering them each a taste or two.

They also tried scallops, short ribs, mushroom risotto, braised duck, clams, prosciutto, gnocchi and an assortment of cheeses.

Everything was delicious and as promised, she didn't feel like she overate and very much enjoyed trying new things.

Cain of course asked if she'd like dessert, which she declined but they both did have coffee to finish their meal.

Becca glanced at the bill and nearly fell out of her chair.

Little dishes are pricey. Hell!

"Worth every penny babe." Since of course, he noticed her expression.

"How about a walk? We can see the lights around the strip." He held out his hand.

She nodded, as she put her hand in his.

He put his jacket around her shoulders.

Once outside the hotel, she was very happy he did since there was a slight breeze and without the sun, the evening had cooled down a bit.

They managed to walk down to the 'Mirage' and watched the volcano erupt before heading back to their room.

A sad note, the volcano would soon be taken out since the 'Mirage' was sold and would eventually become the new 'Hard Rock' casino.

They both enjoyed getting back into the very comfortable bed, to sleep.

Yes, even rabbits need their rest.

TUESDAY

Checking out just before nine that morning, they both admitted to each other about still being very full from their late dinner but definitely needing a caffeine fix.

Becca suggested swinging by 'Dutch Bros.' on the way out of town and Cain handed her back her keys.

"I'll take over driving once we stop for gas since you know the way to coffee." He gave her a quick kiss as they headed to the parking garage.

His new favorite coffee house was now 'Dutch Bros'.

Mission accomplished.

She got him to try his 'Macchiato' with white coffee.

Oh yeah, huge fan.

He also tried her iced 'Annihilator' which was a little too sweet for him, but he liked the flavor. Even said it wasn't bad for sugar-free.

Back on the road with Cain at the wheel. Becca texted Mary to give her their tentative ETA to Ely.

Our two love birds were back on the I-15 heading north and would veer onto Highway 93 about twenty-five minutes outside Vegas.

The trip to Ely as mentioned earlier would be just under four hours.

"I believe you left off with you hiding money for Mary." He glanced over to encourage Becca to continue her tale from the day prior.

"Wow, you're like a dog with a bone." She shook her head before continuing.

"I put money away for just about two and a half years. She became very good at deceiving that horrible man, she was married to. Once in a while, she'd give him the bonus check to keep him from getting suspicious and would always say that bonuses were now paid by check only. He bought it. Still pissed me off that he got all her pay checks." Becca paused and took a long drink of her coffee and then resumed the saga.

"I was at my house in Ely when there was a knock on my door and there, she was… lock, stock and barrel. She'd finally made the decision to move out, quit her job and leave his sorry ass. I was so proud of her. Mary stayed with me for almost five months while she filed for a divorce. We left her money in my name until the paperwork went through, and then I moved the thirty-five thousand dollars, she'd managed to save into her name, which she changed back to her maiden name. She also got a new phone number and cut all ties with everyone they knew as a couple. She made a clean break." She had a huge grin on her face remembering that moment.

Cain squeezed her hand.

"After making the choice to stay in Ely, she found a cute little two-bedroom cottage for sale about four miles from my place and got a job at the Chamber of Commerce. I was still traveling around the state doing sales so, it was actually nice to have her look in on my place on occasion when I was out of town."

"Oh, you asked why I chose Ely. Simple really, it's not as hot as Southern Nevada, and after I rented for a couple of years, I found a nice three-bedroom place on two and a half acres that was fenced and a new build, plus it was within my price range. I had a nice retirement fund from my days at Clear Channel, before I changed to print sales. That is what helped me put a decent down payment on the place, which in turn got me into a fifteen-year mortgage instead of a thirty. Ely is just over a five-hour drive to Reno and as you know, less than four hours to Vegas so, it was a convenient location with all my travels. That and being raised in Northern Idaho, it's nice to see the snow once a year. Sometimes twice. Truth be told, when you first see the town, it doesn't seem to have much to offer but it really is quite charming, and it just sort of grew on me after a time." She paused to finish the last of her coffee and look at her handsome guy.

"Baby, when did you meet Gary? Was it in Ely?" He kissed her hand.

"About a year after Mary moved there. The Chamber was having a mixer for the KGHM copper mine, they had over five hundred employees at the time and were the biggest mine in the area before Kennecott. I was her plus one at most functions, including that one. He was there and was actually hitting on Mary before he started chatting me up. That probably should have been my first clue, but I was flattered, and he wasn't bad looking. I carried quite a few more pounds then and my self-esteem wasn't the best. Anyway, we dated for several months and then he moved in. Just under a year later we got married in Reno." She shook her head.

"Will you ever tell me how bad things got for you?" He was just making the turn from the 93 onto the 318 to continue their journey north.

"He drank a lot in the beginning and wasn't a nice drunk. He never hit me, but words tend to leave deeper scars. At least they seem to for me at least." She made an audible sigh.

"About the time I was thinking about moving on with my life, he got sick. Too much alcohol, too much smoking or too much time in the mines. We never knew what triggered all his issues, but he was sick and getting sicker day-by-day. I was working full time and paying all the bills until he got on disability, which helped take the edge off, but he used most of 'his money' to help his daughters. And for that reason and so many others, I never put him on the deed to the house." She grabbed them both a water and took a drink before continuing.

"Anyway, because of the medications the doctors put him on, he had to quit drinking and smoking and that actually made him meaner."

She never wanted to tell anyone how bad it got. Mary knew and that was enough, but Cain loved her and maybe he'd understand. But maybe he wouldn't.

Could she risk that?

"It was just after Dad died, and I was living in the most negative environment you could possibly imagine. Anything and everything that came out his mouth was vile. It didn't help that my mom wasn't doing very well either, and I couldn't continually go north to see her. She never did come to terms with the loss of my dad. And both my brother and I tried to get her to move closer to one of us, but she refused to leave her home. Jake and even Mark would check on her but they both had full-time jobs and Mark has three kids. So, she spent a lot of time alone." She continued after another sip of water.

"Anyway, around that same time, Mary had a new man in her life so, I was giving her some space to find her own happiness. She deserved that. And she didn't need to take on the shit going on in my world. It was truly the lowest point in my life. I felt so utterly lost and alone. And then I got the call from Jake letting me know that Mom died. My world just bottomed out." She looked over at him. He was watching the road, but she knew he was listening to every word.

"Baby, you were in a loveless marriage and just dealt with the death of your dad. And then your mom so soon after.

Of course, you were depressed. Did you get therapy? Get but on antidepressants? Is that the big secret?" He pulled over in Lund to find a restroom and stretch his legs.

"Pills," and her eyes filled with tears. There she said it, out loud. The shame she carried day in and day out. Wasn't really her fault he was out of the car at the time she made the confession.

He opened her door and pulled her into one of his wonderful bear hugs. And it was in his arms she told him of her attempted suicide years earlier and the therapy she finally did get that helped her regain some focus, and her life.

"Thank you for telling me. But, how close did you come to dying since I've already seen that once, up close and personal, and it nearly crushed me?" He took her face in his hands and wiped away her tears with tender kisses.

"I threw up almost immediately after swallowing the pills. My own body was my savior. Mary yelled at me for weeks. Deservedly so. I was a stupid fool. I hope you can please, please forgive me for being so weak?" She nestled into his arms never wanting him to let her go.

"Nothing to forgive, and you are by no means stupid, weak or a fool. It's back in the past but if you ever feel that lost or low again, I need you to promise that you'll tell me so we can face it head-on together, okay?" He had his stern but sexy look.

She nodded and hugged him tighter.

'How did I get so lucky to find this amazing man.' Her ugly secret was out, and he was still there. Loving her.

Not a lot in Lund, Nevada but they did manage to find a bathroom, and Cain picked up a bag of chips to munch on.

He let Becca drive the last thirty-eight miles.

Her house was just a mile or so outside of town and she was getting excited to get home and show Cain around.

She was also tired of riding in the car. It's much easier when you're not the passenger. And doing all the talking. But still...

'How in the hell did I drive all over this state doing sales? Right, I was twenty-five years younger.' She shook her head at the thought.

They arrived just after one in the afternoon. Cain commented how much he loved all the trees around her place. And his surprise at the terrain difference between southern and northern Nevada.

She liked that it didn't look worse for wear since she'd been away.

Once inside, she noted that Mary had opened a few windows and the place smelled fresh and looked very clean. She owed her best friend big time for making that happen.

She'd cleared out all of her late husband's items months before she went up to the cabin. His daughters had taken a few mementos, and the rest went to charity or the trash.

It was after all, her house.

While she was cleansing both herself, and the house of her late husband, she purchased a brand-new king-size bed right before she left for Idaho. It was a gift to herself. And during the tour, she informed Cain of that as well.

"Nice. We get to christen another bed." His wink made her blush since she'd only had sex in her house for a few years before it all came to a screeching halt and as you're aware… that was well over a decade ago. Plus, it wasn't great sex to begin with.

He picked up on her shy look and pulled her into his arms. "Let's go to bed now baby." And his lips and tongue were in full seduction mode.

Damn!

He was quite a fan of the bamboo sheets, and they had a very nice time breaking in the new bed. Figuratively only.

Cain was massaging Becca's back, and she didn't want to move, it felt amazing; but reality always seems to get in the way of those very special moments you'd like to relish for the rest of your life.

"We have no food in this house. And as much as I'd love to just lay here in your arms the rest of my life. I'm thinking I should make a trip into town for a few essentials." She gave him a quick kiss, and moved like she was getting out of bed.

"Babe, we'll get to that a bit later. I've not had my fill of you yet." He pulled her back and started to kiss her, everywhere.

It didn't take long for Becca to totally forget about anything but her desire for her very voracious man.

'That man and his stamina.' Jeez!

They both must have fallen asleep after that passionate interlude since the knock on the door startled them both awake.

Becca smiled. Kissed Cain. And told him that Mary was more than likely on the other side of that knock.

With a quick smack on her ass, he was up and heading into the bathroom. "Let's not keep her waiting."

She grabbed her robe and went to greet her very best friend.

Becca never got to utter a word before she was grabbed into a vice gripping hug.

"Oh my God, it's you and you're here. I've missed you so much. I brought you some groceries and was thinking of ordering some dinner for you, so you don't have to cook. How long do I have you for? Please tell me you're not leaving right away." Mary was on a roll.

Thinking her ribs might actually cave in from the hug, Becca squeezed Mary just as tight, and she finally broke free to breath.

Smart girl.

"Hi. Missed you too. Would you like to come in and sit and visit for a while?" Becca gave her friend a huge grin.

"Yes, as a matter of fact, I would like that. You want to put some clothes on since you're flashing your tits at me?"

Already mentioned that she could be quite blunt.

Yep. Huge blush from Becca.

She hurried off to her bedroom for clothes.

Mary went out to her car to get the sack of necessities and was met by Cain at the front door who took the bag from her.

Ever the gentleman.

"You're much more handsome in person." And thanked him for his assistance.

"Why thank you Mary. You're quite lovely yourself. And you're most welcome." He smiled Becca's favorite smile.

About that time, she came out of her bedroom fully dressed and made a comment regarding her best friend's blush.

"You two ladies catch up and I'll get our bags out of the car. I would love to take you both to dinner tonight. Your choice." And with that, he was out the door.

"Girl, he's a keeper with a capital 'K'. And he loves you, I can tell." She took her friend's hand and smiled.

Becca led Mary into the living room after putting the few groceries in the fridge, and they proceeded to have a huge catch-up with what had been going on in both their lives over the past several weeks.

Cain stopped in just quick enough to hand Becca the gift bag, she had for her best bud.

True to form, Mary commented on each magnet and then went nuts over the leaded crystal rose with the etched leaves.

Another huge hug and a couple of very happy tears.

"Oh my God you shouldn't have but I'm so glad you did. This is going to go nicely with my collection. Love you Becs."

"It was the least I could do for you keeping an eye on the house and everything. And I love you back."

She also let her friend know that her 'dark secret' that was only known by the two of them was out of the bag with her man.

Mary knew at that moment just how important Cain was to her friend.

Becca was thrilled to find out that Mary and Liam were still a couple when he was in town. Leave it to her to start a new relationship with a long-haul trucker.

New being a tad abstract... she and Liam had been together for just under six years now.

Her reasoning was quite simple. 'He's not underfoot all the time and when they are together it's quite wonderful'.

Something must be working, apparently his stamina is similar to Cain's.

Well Damn!

Maybe they could clone them for the rest of the ladies out there. Just a random thought.

About the only topic that got Mary's hackles up was finding out that her friend and beau were leaving on Thursday to head to Idaho.

"You just got back, and you promised you'd be around for several weeks." She pouted with the best of them.

"It's just for a long weekend. We'll be back." She knew she'd promised but that was before Jake called regarding the surprise birthday party.

"Why don't you come with us? I know you have more than enough leave time since you've not taken a serious vacation for a couple of years now." That idea came very quickly.

"Really? Cain won't mind?" Her inquisitive question made Becca think she might want to ask the love of her life.

The wonderful guy who has made himself scarce for over an hour.

'What a sweetheart'. She smiled to herself.

"If you're worried, I'll be happy to ask him."

Mary acknowledged that she'd feel better with his approval of this new plan.

Becca went and found Cain walking around the property.

"Everything okay my love?" And she reached up to give him a nice kiss hello.

"Yes, my girl. Just looking around and giving you and Mary and chance to catch up." He wrapped her in his arms.

"I want to invite her to come to Idaho with us. Would you be okay with that?" She loved being in his arms.

"What a great idea. Give us time to get to know each other since she's your oldest and dearest friend." He was wearing her smile.

She loved this amazing man so very much.

Becca reached up and brought his lips back to hers and gave him the most passionate thank you kiss she had to give.

"Becca, sweetheart unless you'd like me to take you right back to bed, I would suggest you head back into the house and let me walk off this arousal you've just caused." His questioning look matched hers since she wasn't sure which she'd prefer at that moment.

Well of course that's what she'd prefer but her best friend was waiting in the living room.

Decorum people.

As she turned to leave, he gave her a rather audible smack on her ass.

She was grinning all the way back into the house.

Once back in front of her bestie, "he loved the idea of you coming along. It will give you both a chance to get to know each other better." She paused for a second.

"You know it just occurred to me that it's Tuesday, and you're here and not at work."

"I took the week off so I could spend as much time with you as possible. Not knowing what your plans were and how long I would have you for. Of course, after meeting your guy, I totally get it and understand that I now have to share you. I can do that." She winked.

Awe! What a great and perfect friend.

"Do you think you can take Monday off too since I think that will be the day we drive back from Northern Idaho?"

Mary told Becca that she was sure it would be fine, but she'd check to make sure.

Neither of them realized that Monday was Labor Day, and the Chamber office would be closed.

Cain reappeared. "Ladies, where is a good place to eat around here?"

Mary suggested 'Twin Wok'. And Becca thought 'Cellblock Steakhouse' could be fun.

They left the final decision up to him.

Since they just had sushi the day before, and Chinese the days before that, the choice was easy. And who doesn't like to eat in a makeshift jail.

Weird, but kind of cool.

Mary was going to stop by the Chamber office before dinner and make sure getting Monday off wouldn't be an issue and was going to meet them at the Jailhouse Casino, which is where the restaurant was located.

The plan was set to meet in one hour.

The minute she was out the door, Cain had Becca in his arms, and his lips reminded her of their early moment in the yard.

"Baby, I think you're going to make a very nice appetizer." He led her back into the bedroom and proceeded to work up both their appetites.

Oh, and they were hungry after their interlude too.

Her shower wasn't quite big enough for two but somehow, they managed. Those close quarters almost made them late for dinner.

Damn, that man and his stamina.

Becca did manage to change the sheets, and get the first set into the wash before they left to meet Mary.

Cain was highly amused with the décor' of the restaurant. They actually ate in a jail cell.

He ordered wine for the table and got shrimp cocktails for the three of them as well as chorizo-stuffed mushroom caps. The ladies each chose the 'Rustler', a six-ounce Filet Mignon and Cain went for the Gambler's Prime Rib, a very hearty sixteen-ounce portion.

Excellent food and no one left feeling one bit hungry.

Cain only bitched a little at Becca for not eating any of her rice, but gave it a rest when she finished her whole steak.

Mary couldn't help but laugh letting him know that she was glad someone else was on the job.

It usually fell on her shoulders to get on her friend for not eating.

Becca ignored them both.

Mary also made the comment that Cain looked nothing like an investment broker, cop maybe or lawyer. That got huge laughs. As did the realization that Monday was a national holiday.

It was a very causal and pleasant evening.

Nice to see that her favorite guy and favorite girl could get along so well.

Our two ladies made arrangements for the following day to have lunch while Cain did some work in peace and quiet at the house.

After hugs and good-nights the trio was down to just a duo and they all headed to their prospective homes for a good night's rest.

Becca managed to read two chapters of 'Great Expectations' before they both crashed for some well-needed rest.

WEDNESDAY

They were woken up from a nice sound sleep by a very loud version of 'All My Ex's Live in Texas'.

It would seem that Cain's father was a huge 'George Strait' fan and that was his ringtone.

"Sorry babe, I thought I put it on silent before we went to bed last night. Dad doesn't usually call this early so something must be up." He climbed out of bed and grabbed his phone off the dresser.

She was too tired to even enjoy the view of her half naked man but did note that it was not quite five.

Her focus changed just seconds after Cain answered the phone.

"Hey Dad, what's got you up so early on a Wednesday morning?" His expression went from curious to shock.

"Mom? What's happened? What's wrong?" He put the call on speaker.

Becca along with Cain were now fully awake and concerned.

"Benjamin, your father had a heart attack yesterday afternoon and I need you to come home. He's going in for a triple by-pass tomorrow. Will you come, please." Both he and Becca could hear the anguish in her voice.

"Yes, mom of course I'll come. What hospital is he in? Who's his doctor?" Cain was sitting on the bed holding Becca's hand.

"He's in the cardiac wing at University Hospital and his doctor is Stephen Bailey. I'll be there all day so come straight there from the airport."

"Alright. I'll be there as soon as I can."

She hung up without a good-bye or a 'kiss my ass'.

Relationship is still a bit strained. But then again, her husband just had a heart attack.

And according to Cain the only person on the planet that called him 'Benjamin'. Becca took the hint.

She got up to put on coffee while Cain went to grab a quick shower.

Thank goodness Mary brought those few items to start their day off right. Actually, their day started off shitty, but they'd have caffeine at least.

When he came into the kitchen, he had on just a pair of jeans and was carrying his laptop.

Holy hell that man is gorgeous. Focus!

"Babe, what's the closest airport? And could I ask a huge favor?" He smiled at her since he noticed her gawking at his attire.

"Salt Lake is just under three and half hours and of course I'll do whatever you need. I'm so sorry about your dad. Would you like me to go with you?"

"You have a date in Idaho with your family and even though I would love for you to come with me, I will be happier if you go there. You and Mary can make it a fun girl's trip. And I'll call you every chance I get." He kissed her cheek.

"Would you mind doing a little laundry, so I have clean jeans to pack? I left some items on the floor in the bedroom."

She nodded and handed him a cup of coffee while he perused the airlines for a flight.

After grabbing the two pairs of jeans, three shirts, underwear and his pajama bottoms off the bedroom floor she went and threw the sheets from the washer into the dryer and started a quick wash for Cain.

"Baby what are your thoughts about flying to Spokane and renting a car for your weekend trip? I sort of need to take your car today." He gave her a sheepish smile.

She came and sat next to him at the island with her own cup of coffee before responding.

"I think Mary and I can just use her car to drive up. You go ahead and take mine."

"I don't like you driving that far so I already booked you both on a Delta flight tomorrow morning at eleven-thirty and there is a car on reserve at Budget for you, a sedan." He grinned again.

"Well thank you for asking at least." She couldn't help but laugh.

Still a few traits of 'Fifty'.

She let it go since he really did it to be nice and because he loves her. It's all new but so very sweet.

"When is your flight and would you like some breakfast?"

"Two-twenty today on Delta. Managed to find a direct flight right into San Antonio. And no thank you, still quite full from last night's dinner."

"Okay, well I guess I'll go get in the shower" She rose to leave and he pulled her into his arms.

With his lips and tongue playing with her ear she squirmed. He knew that was a very sensitive location. His hands worked around to her breasts and her moan of approval was all he needed.

Her nightgown got thrown somewhere in the hall. He smacked her ass telling her to get into bed.

Cain climbed in after, minus his jeans.

Their kisses intensified along with their desire for one another.

Her body always comes alive with him near and he slid in two fingers to make sure she was ready for him. As his lips wrapped around one breast and the then the other, his fingers slowly started to ease in and out at a very sensual pace. Her first orgasm hadn't even finished when he pulled his fingers out and filled her with her favorite sex toy. He kept their rhythm slow, and he pushed himself as deep inside her as he could, savoring every thrust and giving them both a very powerful climax.

She would never get tired of loving this man.

"Damn woman, I am going to miss you. Maybe once you're back from Idaho and depending where things are with dad and New York, you can come meet up with me." He gave her a very tender kiss and as he pulled out of her, she felt a twinge, he hadn't made her that sore, that quick, in quite a while.

He cradled her in his arms and she hugged him back.

She would miss him too but was afraid to speak since she didn't want to cry.

Her love for this man was overwhelming her at that moment.

She nodded letting him know that meeting up with him was a very pleasant idea.

Becca had had so many other similar moments in their just over seven-week romance but this seemed extra special, he filled her heart.

They laid in bed until seven-thirty, Cain had to leave by nine for the long drive to the Salt Lake airport and she needed to get his wash in the dryer.

With clean sheets in hand and his wash now in the dryer, he helped her change the bed before she headed into the shower.

Once dressed and in the kitchen, Becca found four hundred dollars in cash on the counter.

'That man!' She couldn't help but shake her head.

"You need to keep your cash Cain. I'm okay but thank you." She handed him back his money.

Huge surprise, he actually took it.

Truth was, if she really needed money, she could get a loan against her house, take out some of her retirement or sell her share of the cabin to Jake. None of those options were necessary at this point in time.

She did however need to go through a mountain of mail.

No time like the present since Cain was busy answering emails and doing his own online bill paying.

She finally noticed he was fully dressed and asked if he wanted a shower before he left. He didn't. He told her he liked having her smell all over him. And winked.

Nice to know he can still shock the living crap out of her.

Back to the task at hand, Becca put the trash can next to her and started to sort her mail. She was quite pleased that a good portion was junk.

Two bank statements to go through. Property taxes and insurance for both her car and house would be due in September so she put those three aside to pay. She needed to go through the charges on her credit card bill since that one was paid directly out of her bank account. And the last bill she had to write a check for was tags for her car. September was turning out to be the harshest month of the year.

Cain finished up his tasks and looked over at the few extra bills that Becca had in her small pile.

"Babe, how much will all that cost?" She knew he was just concerned and not trying to be overly intrusive.

She let him know it was just over thirty-five hundred and once she went through her two bank statements, she'd have a better idea of where she stood.

Becca then asked him not to worry, he had enough on his plate.

She went to see if his clothes were dry. They were, she took them into the bedroom and folded them so he could pack. He only had about a half hour before he needed to take off to the airport.

"Your clothes are folded, on the bed and ready to pack my love." She gave him a quick kiss when she came back into the kitchen.

He gave her one of his bear hugs. "Thank you, baby. I'm going to miss you like crazy."

"Me too, so very much."

He let her go and made his way back to her room to put his suitcase in order.

She went to snag the stack of bills she'd left on the counter and saw a check sitting on top.

'Holy fuck!' He gave her ten-grand, really.

When he came out with his bag, Becca tried to hand him back the over the top, over generous and extravagant check.

"Just deposit it and pay your bills please. I don't want to worry about you too. I love taking care of you, if you hadn't noticed." He gave her a poignant look.

Her look must have been less than grateful, since truth be told, he was frustrating the crap out of her.

She might have accepted a couple thousand but he always took things to the extreme.

Mega extreme if you ask me.

"Becca, do not argue with me about the check. And believe me when I tell you that I will be watching my account to make sure it gets deposited. If it doesn't, I will get really twitchy with you." It was his stern but sexy look.

She shook her head knowing that they had already agreed to no more twitchy palm but loved him for his overly generous nature and agreed to do as he asked.

They walked out to the car hand in hand.

She really hated to see him leave and prayed his dad would be okay.

Cain put his bag and computer in the back seat and pulled her into a very warm embrace followed by a rather intense and stimulating kiss.

"I love you with all my heart and I'll call as soon as I'm in Texas."

"I love you too Cain, so very much. Please drive safely and I hope all goes well with your dad's surgery tomorrow."

As he released her, he gave her one little smack on the ass reminding to go to the bank.

She nodded and watched the love of her life drive away.

Totally sucks out loud.

She called Mary to fill her in on the early morning call from Cain's mom, leaving out the saga that went along with their tumultuous relationship.

And of course, she needed to know about the change in plans for the Idaho trip that now included them flying.

This new itinerary change meant that they would have to leave by seven to get to the airport for their flight to Spokane the following morning.

She was not at all happy about that last bit of information.

Mary isn't exactly a morning person and told Becca that she would be driving them to Utah.

"I can do that and I'll cover the long-term parking for your car and the rental once were in Washington. I'm just glad you're going with me."

"Of course. I don't want you to go alone, again and now we can really have a proper catch up."

Becca asked if she'd mind giving her a ride into town so she could do a bit of banking and pay some bills.

She'd promised her future husband to deposit the check and she didn't want to break that promise. Plus, even if they agreed on the intensity of the smacks on her ass… no need pushing his buttons.

She rather liked the playful smacks.

He'd been gone all of forty minutes or so and she missed him.

Her sigh was audible. She didn't like the idea of him paying for her house and car. She'd paid her own bills for years and years. As sweet as his gesture was, they were going to have to come to terms regarding their financial differences… eventually.

Mary informed her that lunch was on her and she'd pick her up around eleven since she hadn't even gotten in the shower.

Mentioned that she's not a morning person.

Yes, of course Becca agreed to the terms. She didn't have a car. Plus she adored her best friend.

While waiting for her chauffer, she got the deposit ready, wrote the four checks and also organized all the pictures she'd taken in Alaska on her phone.

Our two best buds made a day of getting all their errands done, had lunch and for a nice twist, Mary let Becca take her car home and told her to come back in the morning to pick her up for their trek to the Salt Lake City Airport.

While she had wheels, she decided to finish the gift she'd been planning for Cain.

It was something that was important for her to do alone because it was a way to express the love, she had for him and it was vital to her to keep it just between the two of them.

A quick trip to 'Let's Print' to get copies of the forty or so photo's she'd taken on their trip north.

She'd already chosen the one's that she wanted, which was a chore in itself since she must have taken close to two hundred pictures.

While there, Becca found a photo album that would work just perfect for her gift.

She had been thinking a lot about how to convey to Cain how much she loved him and what the trip to Alaska had meant to her. She decided to incorporate all his notes with the photos.

Before leaving town, she topped off the gas tank, checked the oil and washer fluid.

Finally back home, Becca went about organizing all his precious words and the photos together plus writing her own special comments on each of the pictures. It was like revisiting Alaska all over again.

Yes, she cried but they were happy tears.

Once she got the album finished, she wrapped it up and put the card she picked up for her man at the same time she'd gotten a birthday card for James.

She'd need to pack her brother's birthday gift but Cain's would stay on the kitchen island until they were back from New York.

'Hope you like it my love' and gave the card a kiss before placing it on top of his gift.

Feeling quite proud of herself, she moved on to getting things arranged for what she'd need to take up to Idaho and print she and Mary's boarding passes.

Becca was so used to having her Buick, she tended to over pack but now she had to limit everything to one checked bag, a carryon and her purse.

Hell, it was only for four days… it really shouldn't be that tough.

'SHIT'! She forgot to take her iPod out of the car, again.

Maybe she should think about having one for the house that could work as her spare. Just a thought.

Becca had just closed her suitcase when her cell phone rang letting her know that she had a video chat calling.

It was Cain.

Huge smile since she'd been thinking about him nonstop for the past couple hours.

"Hi Cain. How's your dad?" He looked so handsome, even on the small phone screen.

"Hey baby, you look wonderful and I miss you." He was smiling her favorite smile. "Dad is doing okay he looks really tired and older. I spoke with his doctor and he's quite confident that he can make a full recovery after this surgery tomorrow and that made me feel a lot better. The operation will take around six hours and he'll be in the hospital about a week after but then he can go home and recuperate. That will take anywhere from six to twelve weeks. At this point, I'm thinking of staying here until he gets to go home. Then you and I can come back in a few weeks to check on things."

"That is wonderful news. And I think you should stay for as long as you wish. I'm glad you're there but I miss you here. How are things with your mm?" She almost hated to ask but in the back of her mind she was hoping they could get past, the past.

"We are never going to have a very loving mother and son relationship but she did ask me to stay at the house with her so maybe we can find some sort of middle ground." He shrugged.

"By the way, thank you for banking the check. Did you get everything paid? Are you all packed for tomorrow?" He gave her a wink.

"It was still way too generous but yes as promised I deposit your money. Everything is paid and I just finished packing as your call came in." She smirked at him.

"You know baby, once we're married you are going to have to stop worrying about my money since it will be ours." Very pointed look after that statement.

As mentioned before, she'd thought about this since he asked her and a few times since but had not said anything until now.

"If and when we marry, I think you should have me sign a 'prenup' so your assets are protected."

It just seemed right since his net worth was far greater than her own. She thought it was being fiscally responsible.

WOW! She didn't expect that reaction.

"Are you fucking kidding me right now? Your ass is going to be sore for at least a month if you ever say something that unbelievably stupid again. Do you understand me?" He looked furious.

"Cain, I didn't mean to upset you. But…" He cut her off.

"No buts Becca. No fucking prenup and no bringing it up again. I'll call you later, my mom wants to go have dinner." And with that he ended their video chat.

She felt horrible.

He didn't even say 'love you' at the end.

Ever the button pusher... this was totally different.

She really was trying to do the right thing by him and his finances. How could he not see that.

Not in a million years did she think he would have that kind of reaction. Deal or no deal, she knew he was serious about spanking her.

She also looked at the clock thinking it was early for dinner but he's now in Central Time so it was actually quarter after seven there.

Anyway, she couldn't let this thing hang between them. She texted him an apology and told him, she mentioned the 'p' word out of love and respect for him. And then ended the text with 'I love you with all my heart, hothead'.

It took several minutes but she got a text back that read, 'I love you too, crazy, overthinking woman.'

She couldn't help but laugh since it was a true statement.

Mood changer to be sure.

The knock on the door scared the crap out of her since she had Mary's car and no one else really knew she was home.

'Awe.' Federal Express was there with her four new dresses.

She thanked the driver and went back into the kitchen to find a knife to open the box.

Cain kept with the shorter dress theme and got her a black one with a lovely tree graphic, a grey one with feathers, a rose color dress with butterflies and finally a deep burgundy pixie dress.

'Wow'.

Becca gathered up her new items and went and hung them up in her closest. While she was at it, she hung up all her clothes from her second suitcase that wouldn't be needed until maybe the next trip and did the same for the clothes that Cain left behind.

Seeing his shirts, pants and jackets in her closet made her extremely happy.

She really would be proud to be his wife.

After the trip north and his father's surgery she'd let him know that they should indeed get married in Hawaii in January.

Mary called an hour or so later to check up on her friend and to see if she needed to grab dinner?

Becca declined food since she wasn't that hungry, stress always messed with her, but they chatted for a few minutes about nothing too consequential.

And 'NO' she didn't mention the disagreement with Cain or the proposal. Still trying to find the right words to broach that subject.

What they both decided would be a great idea, a bubble bath so they ended their call to go relax in a vat of hot water.

Mary had one of those old fashion claw tubs that Becca always coveted. She herself would have to settle for her own garden tub.

Thank goodness she found a relaxation therapy bath bomb, her last one. She'd need to order a few more from 'Amazon' when she got back.

Yep, random thoughts amok.

She'd just climbed in the soothing water when her phone rang.

Well of course it did, timing is everything.

She wiped her hands and picked up the phone, it wasn't a number she knew but answered it anyway.

"Hello?"

"Oh, hi Cain." And put it on speaker.

"Hey baby, my phone is on the charger so I'm using Mom and Dad's landline. People still have those apparently." He chuckled.

He sounded so much better.

"My mother wants to head back to the hospital for the evening visitation hour but I wanted to call and hear your voice. What are you doing?"

"I'm currently relaxing in the tub." She knew that would get a reaction.

"And me without video, well that just sucks. We could always have phone sex?"

He knew she was blushing. Doesn't take 'Kreskin' to figure that one out.

"Thanks, but I'm still sore from your earlier prowess." She smiled at the thought.

"Good to hear. Listen babe, I've got to go but I'll call you again if it's not too late. I love you Becca." He sounded so tired.

"I'm two hours behind you so please call before you go to sleep and I love you too." And with that she was back to being alone in her bath.

The soak was nice, but she still felt anxious and actually a little hungry.

Mary brought some eggs and bacon yesterday but that seemed like too much of an effort.

She went into her panty and found a box of 'One' protein bars. Score! The blueberry cobbler has always been her favorite.

She put the kettle on for a cup of tea and took the remaining three bars and put them in her carryon bag to take with her on the trip.

'This time tomorrow I'll be swimming in my lake.' That thought alone made her entire evening.

With a nice cup of hot tea and her favorite meal replacement bar she sat down with her IPad to check her emails and maybe read a few chapters.

Becca was pleased to see one from her nephew Jake.

Hey Aunt Becs,
Thought I'd give you a quick update.
Pops is driving over on Friday and I'm taking him to dinner as part of the rouse. On Saturday he's spending the day with Mark and the kids and on Sunday we are

all going out to the cabin to have the last barbeque of the season.

Justin and I have to work Thursday but then we both have a nice four-day weekend.

When are you and Cain driving up? I thought you said something about coming Friday as well.

Anyway, safe travels and I can't wait to see you both.

Love, Jake

She thought about telling him about the change in plans but decided that she would just surprise him. If he was on the water tomorrow, he'd see the lights at the cabin and stop by.

It would be so much easier to explain everything in person.

Becca couldn't believe she was yawning at quarter to ten at night but then remembered they had been woken up pretty early.

Plus, it had been a very eventful day.

She grabbed her phone changer and headed into the bedroom to get ready for a good night's rest.

Becca had just put on her satin pajama shorts and top when his call came.

Yes, video. Glad you're back to keeping up.

"Hello my love." She had to catch her breath.

He was shirtless.

Damn he's hot!

"Hi babe, looks like you're getting ready for bed. Wish I was there to help you out of that satin ensemble."

"I'd like that too. How's your dad tonight? What time is his surgery tomorrow?"

"So, that would be 'no' to video sex?" He was laughing.

She just shook her head.

One-track 'fucking' mind.

"Thinking it Becca."

She still loved his stern but sexy look and shrugged.

"By the way, do you know why I had an extra two hundred dollars in my jeans pocket? Your infractions are piling up and your ass will pay the price when I see you."

"It was your money anyway so lighten up." She gave him her best 'I adore you look'.

If you're wondering, it was from the envelope that he gave her back on their first day in San Diego when she went shopping with Joel.

He finally smiled. "Dad was about the same. They gave him something to help him sleep just before we left. His surgery is at ten in the morning and I won't know anything before four tomorrow afternoon. That's two your time so I'll more than likely call while you're on the road to the cabin. If you prefer, I can call later."

"No, I'll be thinking of you the entire time so please call as soon as he's out of surgery and in recovery. I'll also let you know when we get to the airport."

"Thank you. The more I hear your voice the better tomorrow will be. By the way, I heard from New York and that meeting is now set for next Thursday. They wanted me to come on Tuesday but I told them about my dad and they agreed to give me the extra couple days."

"Are you still worried about the outcome?" She didn't want him to have any more stress.

"Not now. I can always find another job. Today put several things into prospective for me. As soon as you're back from Idaho, I'll get you a flight to meet me here or there depending on Dad. And one more thing baby, please marry me."

"Cain, I love you and you own my heart, you know this, but with everything going on can we please wait until after your dad's operation?"

He nodded.

"Okay, call me when you get to Salt Lake. Did you get some cash for the trip? Do you have everything you need?"

"Yes, I got cash and the only thing I forgot was to pull my iPod out of the damn car."

"Babe, you're going to long term parking tomorrow, just grab it when you get to the airport. Didn't you mention having a hide-a-key on the car? I parked it on the third floor about half way down."

He's brilliant, she just smiled since it hadn't even occurred to her.

His yawn caused a chain reaction and she followed suit. They said their goodnights and he did offer video sex once more but she kindly took a rain check.

After they had said their 'love yous' they both put their phones down but didn't hang up. He didn't want to sleep without her and she was in complete agreement.

Becca made the conscious choice to not tell him the dresses arrived. She was sure he would want her to model them and truth be told, she was just too tired. And that might have led to him wanting video sex, again. She'd wait for the real thing.

After stacking the pillows in such a way that she had something to hold throughout the night she put her phone next to her head and listened to Cain breathing.

Yep, she really missed her man.

THURSDAY

Her alarm went off at five-thirty, too damn early. Her phone was still next to her, but the screen was blank. Sometime during the night, their call must have ended. Still, she slept well with him next to her in some sort of fashion.

Becca got up to take a quick shower to rinse-off her sleep and had plans to drink copious amounts of coffee before she headed over to pick up Mary for the first leg of their road trip.

If Mary was true to form, she'd sleep the better part of the three-plus hour drive.

As she poured her first cup of coffee, she put a reminder in her phone to pick up her iPod when she got to the airport. She didn't want to forget her music source for a third time.

It's the little things that can make one smile.

When her phone rang, she figured it was Mary but to her delight, it was Cain.

He must be at the hospital by now since he didn't video chat.

She answered on speaker so, she could consume more coffee.

"Good morning my love."

"Hey babe. I just wanted to hear your voice before you left for the airport. What time are you girls taking off?"

"I'll head out of here in about a half hour to go and roust Mary. We should be on the road by seven. How's your father doing this morning?"

"As good as to be expected. He had a restful night. They are going to prep him for surgery in about an hour. Make sure you're giving yourself enough time. I don't want you to have to speed."

"Please don't worry about me. You have enough on your plate. Besides that, it's not my first time driving to an airport, and you already know that I like to push the suggested speed limit." She was totally trying to lighten his mood and maybe point out his overbearing ways.

"Becca, I will always worry about you. So, call me when you get to Salt Lake, drive safe, and I love you."

"I will and I promise to be careful. Your dad will be in my prayers all day, and you as always will be in my heart."

No more than a second after her call ended with Cain, she was startled by another call. This one was from Mary.

"I'm up and I hate both you and your fella for this way too early departure time." She yawned.

"Well good morning to you too grumpy. I'll pick you up in less than a half hour so get in the shower and get dressed. Do I need to bring you coffee?"

Becca was so messing with her bestie.

"YES!" And with that, the phone went dead.

So not, a morning person. She couldn't help but laugh out loud.

Mary was the one person in the world that Becca could depend on and be herself with… until Cain came along.

As promised, she went and grabbed two travel mugs and filled them both leaving room for cream. Thank goodness they took their coffee the same exact way. Easier to remember.

'Okay, the car is all packed, coffee on board and I'm leaving my house again. So strange being back. But even more strange to be leaving again after less than two days.' With that internal dialogue complete, she locked the front door and headed to go get her friend.

As predicted, Mary slept almost the entire trip to the airport.

Becca drank both coffees.

Snooze you lose.

Once in long-term parking, she managed to find her Enclave without too much difficulty and snagged her iPod. She locked both cars and threw her spare key into her bag and gave Mary back hers.

It was only a quarter to ten, so they'd made really good time and had well over an hour and a half before their flight.

Or not!

'FUCK'. They totally forgot that Utah was in 'Mountain Time Zone', and they had to get their asses down to Delta Airlines to check their bags and get their gate, ASAP.

On route, she texted Cain that they'd arrived, and she'd call him once she was through security.

He was quick to send her a happy face and six red hearts.

Mary commented on her smile. She grinned even bigger.

Never fails when you're in a hurry… their flight was leaving from the farthest gate possible.

'AGAIN, FUCK!'

They each had their one carryon and one personal item, for them, they each had a purse.

Security took forever. Never good when you're in a hurry.

Fucking little 'Nazis' actually made her take-off her 'lovebird' ring and her gold earrings that were a gift from Mary a few years prior. She put them all in the little velvet bag that also contained her mom's diamond earrings.

Safely stowed in her purse, she was finally released from TSA's clutches.

The ladies picked up water on their hike to the outermost corner of the Salt Lake City airport since all this rushing was making them sweat.

Even Mary was making snide comments.

This actually amused Becca and her mood lightened up quite a bit.

Her bestie had a very wicked sense of humor.

One she appreciated so very much.

Especially at that stressful moment.

She apparently was taking too long in calling Cain since her phone started ringing halfway to the gate.

"Hi... nope still got a bit of a walk before we arrive at our departure destination." She chuckled since the whole situation was beyond crazy.

She listened as he said something about cutting the timing close on the flight, and she confessed to sort of forgetting the time zone difference.

She was glad he didn't give her a lecture about that but instead told her about the prep they had to do on his dad before his triple bypass and trying to calm his mother, who broke down the minute he was wheeled out of the room.

She knew that she would totally be a basket case if it were him.

"You holding up, okay? I wish I'd come with you."

He told her that she was where, she was supposed to be and to call when she landed in Spokane.

With good-byes and 'love yous their call ended.

"You two are beyond sickeningly in love. I'm so happy for you and jealous as all hell." Mary gave her a hug since Becca really looked like she could use one.

She did.

They didn't have to wait long once they reached their gate. They had already started early boarding.

Becca had just enough time to run to the ladies' room. Lots of coffee.

As soon as the Delta staff announced their rows could finally board, they got in line.

If you're wondering, last minute tickets suck. You pretty much have to take what seats are left so both Becca and Mary were in middle seats in two different rows.

"This is me. Good flight my friend."

Mary stuck her tongue out and headed back two more rows.

'WOW… talk about being in the back of the bus.'

The young man sitting next to Becca offered to move so they could sit together but he had really long legs, which is probably why he chose the aisle seat, she thanked him but told him they would be fine on such a short flight.

Never say things like that.

Jinx!

About that same time, they announced their departure would be delayed by fifteen to twenty minutes as they needed to wait for connecting passengers from another flight.

Probably the best thing that could have happened since now their luggage might actually make the same flight.

She let Cain know of the holdup since he tended to freak… just a bit.

He sent an unhappy face with a thank you for keeping him in the loop.

Becca turned off her phone to save the battery and got out her earbuds to listen to some music.

She liked that all her belongings fit nicely under the seat in front of her. No disturbing her row companions and easy access.

That made her smile and miss Cain a little more.

It was after all, his favorite statement to her.

She also grabbed a 'One' bar since she'd not eaten anything and had a bad case of coffee stomach. Six cups were definitely overkill. Ick!

The one silver lining about sitting without her bestie and her honey. Nobody to bitch at her about proper eating.

Her neighbor tapped her on the shoulder to get her attention. She only jumped slightly.

Mary was staring at her from the aisle.

Becca pulled out one of her ear buds.

"You have an extra protein bar? I'm starving." Her friend gave her a smile letting her know that she wasn't at all in trouble.

She nodded and pulled another out of her bag.

See, foresight is in fact a very good thing.

Mary thanked her and let her know that they would be having a proper lunch once they landed.

Becca concurred.

Once airborne and allowed to use electronic devices, Becca was back listening to music and fell asleep a few minutes later.

Yep, even with all that caffeine. She is a freak of nature.

The nice tall man next to her woke her as they started their descent into the Spokane International Airport.

She stowed her iPod and earbuds back into her purse and waited to land.

No use getting in an all-fire hurry to exit since the entire plane had to vacate before it would be their turn.

Neither one of her row buddies were overly anxious and that was nice since it took a good ten minutes before they could stand and leave.

Once in the terminal, she and Mary joined back up and headed to the rental cars.

Becca was thrilled that this was a much smaller airport and took no time at all before they were in another line, this one at Budget Rental.

While Mary ran to the restroom and went to retrieve their checked bags, Becca turned her cell phone back on, only to find a missed call from Cain and a text asking where she was?

Mentioned earlier that he tended to freak out... a bit.

She texted back that it takes a while to get-off a plane when you're seated in steerage, and that she was waiting in line to get a rental car.

He sent back an 'lol' and asked her to call him, before she set off to drive to the cabin.

Mary arrived back with their luggage just as she was chatting with the very helpful Budget representative regarding upgrading to a premium or luxury sedan. They both decided to stick with the more affordable intermediate size since it really was just wheels under their butts. That and they were only going to be driving to the cabin and back.

Cain reserved it under her name but on his credit card, and she asked that they put all the charges on her card instead.

Mentioned before. Button pusher extraordinaire. Maybe bumper stickers to go along with the t-shirts.

But seriously, she felt since he gave her that 'way over the top' check, it was the least she could do.

It's not like she didn't have the funds to pay the bill.

With keys and bags, they headed out to find their ride and go get some lunch.

But first, she needed to call her wonderful handsome man.

Mary actually rolled her eyes.

Becca stood outside their silver sedan and did a video chat since she really wanted to see his face.

"Hey, babe it's great to see you." He was wearing her smile. But that's not what got her attention.

"Hi. I know I have a very small screen but are you in a bathroom?" She couldn't help but shake her head.

"Yes, my dad's. Just using it for privacy since my mother is sitting in the room." He again smiled her smile.

She nodded.

"Any issues with them using my card?"

'Fucking 'Kreskin' strikes again.' She was tempted to do her own eyeroll but refrained.

"I just put in on my card since I was the only one here to sign the paperwork." She hoped he'd just let it go.

"Sure, makes sense. Although, I really wish I was there. This waiting around here is killing me. We still won't know anything for another hour or so."

"Please call me the minute he's in recovery and doing okay. You know what the reception is like at the lake. Mary and I are planning to grab lunch before we head out. I love you Cain with all my heart."

"Love you too baby and I'll call as soon as I hear anything. Enjoy your time with your bestie. Glad to see you're not living on protein bars."

Yep, his stern but sexy look.

She shook her head.

It was sad to end the call since she really wanted to give him a hug.

When Becca got behind the wheel, Mary showed her a map quest for 'Izumi Sushi Bar and Asian Bistro' on Regal Street.

She had to smile since they always got sushi when they went to lunch in Vegas.

It was the perfect choice.

"Okay co-pilot, give me directions as we go." She was so glad Mary came with her. She'd missed her a lot more than she'd realized.

On the way to the restaurant, she filled her friend in on everything going on with Cain's dad and about the upcoming trip to New York that she'd be going on with him. And to her surprise, Mary was okay with that trip.

Still not sure how to tell her about the Hawaii trip or the marriage proposal, she decided to leave that for the trip home.

Mary knew her way too well.

"Are you planning on selling your home in Ely and living wherever the yacht is? I can't remember its name." It was a fair question.

"Her name is 'SIRA', and we haven't really discussed it. Cain loves the Nevada house and it's paid for so I'm thinking of keeping it. Besides that, you're there." She gave her best friend a wink and smile.

"Damn straight I'm there. Good, I hate the idea of you moving away."

They were out of the car and heading into lunch when Becca mentioned that the sedan had much touchier brakes than her Enclave or Mary's Equinox.

That and she hated sitting so low to the ground. She now wished they had upgraded.

Woulda. Coulda. Shoulda.

They made short work of ordering three different rolls to share,

'The Spice Girl' and 'The Fire Roll' and to tone things down just a bit, they got 'Godzilla'. It's a very good thing that our two friends both liked a bit of spice.

Now full from lunch, the girls headed back onto the I-90 to start their hour and a half plus drive towards the lake.

They'd just made the turn onto highway 95 heading north when Becca's phone rang.

Mary was nice enough to answer it on speaker.

"Hi Cain, it's Mary. You're on speaker so Becs can hear."

"Okay, thanks. How are you ladies doing?"

In unison they both said fine.

"Good. I wanted to let you know that Dad came through surgery just fine and the doctor said, it went very well and holds to his original thought about him making a full recovery."

"That's great news. The best. I'll call you later tonight. I love you."

"Love you too baby."

"It's sort of sudden since we just met but love you." Mary was laughing.

Becca smacked her friend with the back of her hand since they were currently at a red light in Coeur d'Alene, Idaho.

"Ouch. I'll have you know your girlfriend just hit me." She smirked at her friend.

"Fiancée. Drive safe my girl and call me the minute you get settled at the lake." And he hung up.

'Damn you Cain, fucking instigator'. Snarky in thought only.

Becca concentrated on driving since she knew her friend was boring a hole in the side of her head with the glare she was getting.

"Something you want to tell me? Like the fact you're getting married, and you have not said one fucking word about that."

Yep, she was pissed and mildly hurt.

"Okay. Well, he did ask but I haven't actually said yes, yet. Don't be mad, I was going to talk to you about it over the weekend." She was so hoping that there would be no prying follow-up questions.

"Fine, but we will be chatting at the cabin, and it will be a nice long chat missy."

She knew that tone and nodded.

They didn't speak for about fifteen minutes.

As they passed 'Silverwood Theme Park', Mary commented on the wooden roller coaster. Her friend was quite the daredevil.

Becca still remembered when she went on the ride that tips you 'over the side' on top of the Stratosphere and then there was the zipline down the Rio she went on. Lunatic!

And 'NO' Becca was a mere spectator to both those events.

"Will we have time to go there? Looks like a blast and I counted at least five roller coasters." Her eyes were bright with excitement.

"Maybe. We have no plans for Saturday. I think this might be their last weekend of the season. If that's the case it's going to be very crowded, so keep that in mind."

Mary clapped.

How could she refuse her best friend a trip to an amusement park? Plus, if they went on Saturday, she could have the JJ's come along so, she didn't have to ride any of those damn coasters. Not her thing.

Both their moods were much improved.

It was only twenty-five minutes later when Becca made the turn to head towards the lake road.

They were getting close, and she was excited to show her friend where she'd spent the better part of her youth.

It didn't take long before they were on the dirt road that would take them to the cabin. The sedan handled the paved road and all its curves quite well, but it didn't seem to be as accommodating on the dirt and gravel road that led to the lake house.

It also didn't help that traffic on that part of the drive had grown quite a bit over the past five to ten years so, Becca was really hoping the weekenders wouldn't start arriving until the next day. They tended to be crazy scary on this part of the drive.

Mary was oblivious to the road conditions, looking at the scenery. As soon as the lake appeared through the trees she was in complete awe.

"Oh my God Becs, it's stunningly beautiful. I see the draw for you to come back year after year. Thank you for letting me join you on this trip."

She gave her friend a huge smile. "I do love my lake. There is a spot coming up where the trees thin out a bit, and you can really see how big it is. And no need for thanks, I'm thrilled you're with me."

In case you're curious, Becca had asked Mary to join her a few times, but summer was the busy season for the Chamber of Commerce in Ely, and they asked all their employees to refrain from vacations during that time of the year.

She loved being back and loved showing her best friend her lake.

It was two blind turns later when a black SUV was taking up the whole road and going way too fast for Becca to do anything but swerve to avoid a head-on collision. She applied the brakes and the car's tires didn't grip the road very well and they started to slide on the gravel. It was a knee-jerk decision, and the edge of the road was too close to avoid as the SUV sideswiped their car and nudged them over the embankment.

In what seemed like slow motion they went over the steep terrain.

She heard Mary scream as the car rolled.

Becca felt a sharp pain.

Then nothing... her world went dark!

RECOVERY

When Becca woke, she had a monster headache and couldn't move her left arm.

She also discovered, quite quickly, that breathing seemed to be a bit of an issue. She could take shallow breaths only.

'That's not good.'

Actually, she hurt all over, once she took stock of how her whole body felt.

'What the fuck'?

Once fully conscious and taking in her surroundings she realized that she was in a hospital. 'SHIT'.

Her left arm was in a cast. And so was her left leg. 'Double SHIT!'

Well, at least that explains the movement issue.

But it was her damn head that hurt like a son of a bitch.

She had a stupid IV in her right arm and that too was making it difficult to move.

When she glanced farther to her right… 'Ouch!' She saw James, asleep in the chair next to her bed.

She tried to speak but nothing came out. Her throat was raw and dry, desert dry. 'Fuck me'!

The call button was the only thing, she could reach with a single finger, so she pressed it.

The nurse who rushed in, looked quite surprised when Becca mouthed water. "Welcome back Mrs. Jackson, I'm Hollie, one of your nurses here in ICU. I need to go and inform your doctors that you're awake and I'll also bring you in a cup of ice chips."

Becca nodded... sort of. Hell, even that hurt. 'Again, FUCK'.

Hollie looked to be in her late twenties with blond hair that she put in a ponytail. Pretty blue eyes and curves in all the right places for her five-foot-nothing frame. Becca was a tad jealous, not so much for her cuteness, more because she was mobile.

'But wait... Doctors... how many doctors does one person need?'

"Hey Sis." James stood and gave her a tender kiss on her forehead. She felt a drop of water and realized that he was crying. This made Becca tear up instantly. Her brother was one of the strongest people she knew, and he didn't cry very often. Plus, they hadn't really spoken much in the last two years. So, seeing him that upset made her heart hurt and heal a bit at the same time, just because he was there.

He looked tired and thinner plus he had a beard. She couldn't remember the last time she saw him with facial hair. Not his best look.

"I am so glad to see your eyes open. We thought we'd lost you twice already. I've never prayed so much in my life. You've aged me by ten years. I couldn't take losing you Becs. Do you remember anything about your car accident?"

She shook her head a tad and again, 'Ouch!'

Her moan was the only thing audible.

'Holy shit! A car accident. Really! When? How?' Her thoughts were scattered across the board.

"Okay, well you remember where the osprey nest used to be as you're driving out on the cabin road?" She nodded, only slightly.

"That's were a fucking weekender sideswiped you right off the road. You rolled the car several times before a big pine stopped your descent. That's actually what saved you." He sighed and wiped his tears away. He also dabbed her eyes ever so gently.

She knew that road like the back of her hand. Embankment was a huge understatement. It was a sheer drop-off.

Her eyes were huge at this point.

"Yeah. It was bad. Really bad. A hundred yards either way and you'd have walked away. Jake was the one who found you, and he thought you were dead. Justin was in the sheriff's boat and from his angle, he didn't think anyone could have survived. The car looked more like a taco shell wrapped around the tree." He winced like that hurt to say.

"You've aged them both about twenty years." He just stared at her for a few seconds before continuing.

"Bonner General hospital got you as stable as they could and then had you airlifted to 'Deaconess Hospital's trauma center' here in Spokane. Hell, there was even talk of sending you over to 'Harborview' in Seattle." He paused to talk a deep breath.

"You've been in a coma just under two weeks now. Traumatic brain injury is what your neurologist told me. Your brain was swelling, and it had two serious bleeds. That's why they came close to sending you to Seattle. Your orthopaedic surgeon put your arm and leg back together. Compound fractures to both your left arm and left leg. Plus, four broken ribs, a broken nose, a fractured left cheek and too many bruises, cuts and contusions to count. Oh, and you no longer have a spleen." He reached and held her right hand giving it a tender squeeze.

It felt nice and warm and hers was cold. His retelling of her injuries sent a bigger chill down her spine.

'I must look like a hot mess.' Passing thought.

One thing she knew for sure, she felt like total shit. Everything hurt.

They were interrupted by two doctors and the nice nurse Hollie, who handed James the cup of ice chips.

He put one piece in Becca's mouth, and it felt wondrous.

Who knew a simple shard of frozen water could taste that incredible?

'Fuck, it even hurt like hell to smile.'

Yep. Hot Mess!

"Hello Rebecca, I'm Dr Lawson, your primary here at the hospital. Are you in pain?" She gave a little nod.

He was young, clean-shaven, short brown hair with kind hazel eyes and looked about James' height of five foot ten.

"That's to be expected. We removed your breathing tube yesterday after your brain stopped swelling so, I would imagine your throat feels a bit dry and raw. How's the headache?"

James gave her another piece of ice and told the nice attending that, she preferred to be called Becca.

She squeezed his hand to say a nonverbal thank you.

"I'll make a note in your chart. Now, how's your head?"

She couldn't speak very well, so with barely a whisper she answered his question. "Hurts".

"Thought it might. We're going to give you some pain medication in your IV. And I am sure you have lots of questions but for now we really just want you to get as much rest as possible." He had a very kind bedside manner.

She liked him.

The second doctor not so much.

His name was Dr Gering and apparently was the surgeon who patched up her arm and leg.

He was blunt, which she appreciated but he spoke more to her brother, and it made her feel like she wasn't there.

'Arrogant fucker'.

He was older than Dr Lawson, thinner and not in a good way, had jet black hair that was too long for a doctor and pale blue eyes that didn't give much away.

He looked to be an inch or so over six foot. Not unattractive but his bedside manner made him a troll in Becca's eyes.

The nurse was back and injected something into her IV and the fog came on quickly. She barely had time to register Jake's arrival. "Aunt Becs..."

'Oh, shit was he crying'.

She didn't know how long she was out after those kickass meds were given to her and her throat still felt horrid, but her headache had subsided a bit. Small favors.

Breathing was still a challenge. Broken ribs... she winced.

'Was it still the same day?'

'What were the names of those two doctors?'

Brain injuries truly suck!

She looked over and saw that Jake was sitting where her brother was earlier, and he was reading the local paper, 'Spokesman Review'.

Sports section she would guess.

She tried to smile, but that still hurt too much.

"Hi" it was a quiet whisper, but he heard her.

"Hey Aunt Becs, I just want to thank you for scaring the living shit out of me and aging me beyond my years." He bent down and gave her a kiss on her cheek.

"But I 'Thank God' you're back with the living. I had serious doubts about a week and a half ago. So, did Pops. I have never seen him cry so hard when the doctors told him that it was in 'God's Hands' now. Mark was even here then, and he lost it, big time. He couldn't bear the thought of you dying and him not being able to make-up with you. He hasn't been back but that's more because of his dental practice and his stupid wife. I've shed a tear or two myself. The world is a better place with you in it. I love you so much Becs. I am so beyond grateful that you're a fighter."

She teared up, as he spoke and wanted to give him a hug, but her body wasn't going to cooperate with that. She did mouth an 'I love you too'.

What was really plaguing her thoughts was how pale and gaunt he looked, like her brother and he too had a nice beard growing. He looked good with facial hair. Random thought, again.

Her look of concern was not lost on her ever-observant cop nephew.

"Yes, Aunt Becca, I'm well aware I look like shit. So, does Pops but we've been a tad preoccupied worrying about your ass. We've all taken shifts, so you were never alone." He picked up the cup and put an ice chip in her mouth.

How could she not love the little shit?

"Accident?" She wanted him to tell her more.

Just the thought of it made tears well up in his eyes.

Of course, that made her cry too.

'Oh, for the love of God, not again'.

Her emotions were seriously all over the map.

"It was so bad Becs... I really didn't think anyone could survive that drop and then when I found out that it was you. My heart sank. It was honestly the worst day of my entire life." He wiped his eyes and hers.

"The jerk that sideswiped you at least had the decency to call in the accident he caused. No alcohol was involved, just going way too fast and misjudging the curve. Fucking weekenders. My guess is you barely had time to react before you were pushed over the edge." He closed his eyes and took a deep breath.

"Anyway, Justin and I were on the water side of the wreck and spotted the car. Using binoculars, we were able to radio in the license plate and it came back as a rental car. So, our first thought was another weekender since it was three days before Labor Day but then dispatch came back and told us the car was registered in your name." His tears streamed down his face, and she again so wanted to hug her nephew.

"Justin put our boat on the shore, and I bolted up to you as fast as I could. I had to get to you and find out if you were still alive. J stayed and radioed for more help to come from above since we didn't know at that point if it was a rescue or a recovery." Jake was white as a ghost as he retold her of the incident.

"Becs, you were twisted in ways a human body shouldn't be and there was blood everywhere. I really did think you were dead, and I lost it. First time I've ever gotten sick at any accident scene. But then you moaned and all I could do was thank 'God'." He squeezed her hand.

"After letting Justin know that it was a rescue and you were in bad shape, I had him send for the EMT's to come from the water side since it was the quickest way to get you to town. My adrenaline kicked into high gear so some of the details are blurry since I was on autopilot, but it still took us hours to get you out of the wreck, stabilized and onto a trauma board and down to the beach. The 'Jaws of Life' lived up to its name that day. You never spoke and again, I thanked 'God' that you remained unconscious through the whole ordeal since I know we hurt you. A lot!"

She squeezed his hand back.

"Saved." Her voice still a whisper.

"It was a group effort to be sure. But yes, in the end, we saved you." His relief was almost visible.

He looked up and wiped his eyes when James walked back into the room. He handed his son a cup of coffee and sandwich and retook his former chair.

They never spoke, but the love emanating from them was surreal.

She knew they'd been doing this for a couple weeks now and she hated being such a bother but loved them for being with her.

She couldn't see Jake anymore so, she figured there was another chair behind her.

Moving her head was still not the easiest of tasks.

James put another ice chip in her mouth. And held her hand.

"Sorry." It was a quiet apology, but she hated being the one causing them both so much distress and concern.

"You have nothing to be sorry for sis. Nothing!" He leaned over and kissed her hand.

"In fact, I should be the one apologizing and telling you how sorry I am for not believing you two years ago. I've spent too much time trying to appease Mark's wife, and I lost all that time with my only sister. And almost losing you forever made me realize how stupid I was. Will you please forgive me?" He reached over and wiped her tears away.

She managed a weak, 'yes'.

"I love you Sis with all my heart. Let's never fight again, please." And put another ice chip in her mouth.

"Love you," was another whisper, but he heard her.

Jake's "about fucking time" made her smile.

And yes, it hurt but she didn't care, her relationship with her brother was restored.

Ignoring his son, James continued, "By the way, I did reach out to Dad's former attorney, and he'd like to sue the guy who caused your wreck for six or seven figures if you want. His insurance is covering all your medical, and I'm sure they are going to give you some kind of settlement for being out of work for the next several months. But it's not enough. That's why I called his law office after I knew you were stable."

She shook her head a tiny bit, anymore would be too painful.

Let's be clear, Becca can be as vindictive as the next person; in fact, she prides herself on grudge holding, if you've been paying attention.

But, at that moment in time, she was just glad to be alive.

And more than money, she just wanted her body and mind to heal.

With everything Jake told her, and what the doctors told her, she still felt something was missing and she couldn't quite figure out what. But it made her heart ache.

Her head was still quite fuzzy when it came to details, and she didn't remember much prior to the accident. 'And why was I on the cabin road in September? It was September, right?' Brain injuries really do mess you up.

She'd try to remember to ask Jake or James.

The doctors and nurses would quiz her on her name, birthday, who was president and shit like that, but it was the past three or four months that seemed to elude her.

Hell, she couldn't even recall what day it was or which month they were in. As stated earlier.

Although if she was told, she could tell them the information back, even several hours later.

Apparently, that was a good sign.

However, when they asked her what her home address was, she didn't have a clue.

Although that came back after a couple days.

It was very scary all the same.

She hoped with time her brain would reveal her memories. Especially short-term since long-term didn't seem to be a problem.

The nurses were back regularly with more medication, and she knew sleep would soon take her away from her family. It was both good and bad.

The next few days in ICU were much the same. Doctors came and went. She was poked and prodded and the nurses, as stated, kept the kick-ass drugs coming so she slept, A lot!

But the 'black hole' that was her mind was ever present and quite frustrating.

Her throat was getting better each day, and she managed to drink some broth and both her brother, and nephew were being overly attentive.

She woke once to them arguing about telling her some bad news or wondering if they hinted would she remember. When they realized she was awake they changed the subject and wouldn't answer her inquiry.

She did try to get them to go home at one point, but they paid her no mind.

If she were honest with herself, she wasn't quite ready to be alone and their presence every time, she was awake brought her comfort and peace of mind.

Her memories were still out of sorts, which was both daunting and incredibly exasperating.

When Becca woke on day five or maybe it was six from coming out of the coma, she was greeted by a very happy Justin.

"Morning Becca. Damn it's good to see you awake." His eyes glistened with tears, but he kept them at bay as he kissed her cheek.

"Hey J. Did you get called in to give the two stubborn members of the family a much-needed break?" She smiled at her adopted nephew.

"When has Jake ever listened to me. Let alone James. No, your brother is off getting a shower and a change of clothes and Jake is asleep on the couch behind you. He won't leave you. Hell, he even flew in the Medevac that brought you here." Becca couldn't help but cry at the thought of her loving family going through so much hell because of her.

Justin too looked thinner but no beard. She was feeling more of a burden. "I'm so sorry J."

He took her hand and gave it a loving squeeze. "Don't you dare apologize, we're family and that's what you do when one member is hurt. You welcomed me as part of this clan since I was a kid and I love you all for that. Anyone of us would move heaven and earth for you not to be hurt like you are. And we're not going anywhere, you hear me." His tone reminded her of someone. And he was wiping her tears away.

Damn, she loved all the men in her family. And chuckled when her, now awake, nephew put in his two cents. Ribs protested quite a bit.

"Well said my brother from a different mother." She knew Jake was giving his best friend a huge grin.

They all turned when James arrived back with food. He treated himself and the boys to Arby's and brought Becca a smoothie that was the best thing she'd ever tasted.

The coolness did wonderful things to her healing throat.

She was also glad to see them all eat a hot meal of sorts. She was smiling, which didn't hurt as much, as she listened to their banter and reminded herself how lucky she was.

Hollie came in shortly after and put the night-night juice in her IV. Even though it was only late morning.

Becca couldn't object since her whole body was still one big ache.

Just as the drugs were taking affect, she thought she overheard Jake talking to his two companions on the couch.

"Has she said anything about Cain? He has to be worried sick. And the police will come soon and talk to her about the accident. What if they tell her about the death? It will crush her. She just needs to heal. I'm still really worried."

As usual, she wasn't quite sure what day it was when she woke, but it was dark outside, and the room was empty for the very first time.

Becca felt more alone than ever before.

She knew it was selfish, but she was always so thrilled when James, Jake or Justin were there with her when she was awake. They had lives to return to, she would eventually have to put her big girl panties on and let them go.

That and convince them she was ready for them to leave.

Even if she wasn't.

'What was Jake saying earlier in the day? Or was it even the same day?' She couldn't quite remember.

Head injuries totally blow.

She could see just fine with the help from the light in the hall and for the first time she got up the nerve and gingerly lifted her bed sheet with her right hand, minding the IV of course.

Her right leg looked like one big bruise, but she could wiggle her toes.

Again, and again it's the little things that can make one happy.

She had finally remembered that she lived in Nevada but still missed Alaska so very much. But she couldn't remember where she lived or if she lived there. She was however sure she'd been.

She kept telling herself, 'Baby steps Becs'
Still sucks out loud.

She recalled her parents passing away a few years back and leaving her and her brother a small inheritance and the cabin to share.

Her childhood memories were all there and easy to bring forward, but she couldn't remember the last few months. Beyond vexing!

She recollected divorcing that horrible man she married. 'No, that's not right, he died'.

'Wow! I seriously have a fucked-up brain.' It felt so alien to have blanks in her life.

She also smiled thinking that she wasn't supposed to say the word 'Fuck'. But had no idea why.

She happened to like the word. Versatile in so many ways; being a noun, adjective, expletive and verb.

Becca tended to veer a lot these days. Brain mush.

She did remember spreading ashes. But whose?

Her best friends? 'No!'

Mary was alive, she was sure of that. But there was something about Mary, she needed to remember. She almost had her mobile phone number figured out and would call and see if she could fill in the gaps.

Cell phones are good and bad since everyone tends to rely on them to remember important details like phone numbers.

Still, she wanted to talk to Mary since best friends always know all the answers.

'Maybe Jake could find my cell'.

She was keeping a running list in her head. She only hoped it didn't leak out somewhere.

Trust me that was a concern at this point.

She very much hated that the last several months remained black holes.

Something was missing, and it was causing her to grieve for a loss she didn't understand. But it wasn't for her husband. Their marriage wasn't the happiest. That at least she did know.

Hollie, the very sweet nurse was back that evening and handed Becca a popsicle. "I know your throat is getting better. But who doesn't like popsicles?" She had a nice smile.

Becca grinned since anything cold still helped and felt amazing. And thanked her favorite nurse.

"I'm off shift, but Sara and Adam will be here to take care of you for the rest of the evening and throughout the night." She patted Becca's hand.

As she departed, Becca's third doctor walked in. He was older than the other two with a full beard. He had salt and pepper colored hair and very flattering brown eyes. A bit shorter than James but on the whole attractive.

"Hello Mrs. Jackson, I'm Peter Jarvis, your neurosurgeon. We met three days ago but only briefly and I didn't know if you would remember me." She nodded since she actually did.

"Well, I must say; you gave me quite a run for my money these past few weeks. I'm very pleased to see you looking more alert. How are the headaches these past couple days?"

"Becca please, and they are getting a little better each day."

"Well Becca I'm glad to hear it, but I don't want you to be brave, if you need pain meds, please just ask. What your body needs more than anything is rest. And lots of it."

That's what Dr Lawson keeps telling her as well. 'All I do is sleep' was her main thought as she looked at the attentive Neurosurgeon.

"Are you able to taste the flavor of the popsicle?" She liked his smile, but what an odd question.

She nodded and asked why?

Apparently, twenty-five percent of people who suffer brain injuries lose their taste buds and their ability to smell. The two senses kind of go hand-in-hand. But even with her broken nose, she could still smell and taste.

Again… small favors.

She had more than enough shit wrong with her.

Dr Jarvis proceeded to shine a light in both eyes and move her head a bit which didn't exactly feel great, but he did his best not to hurt her either.

He went on to tell her how lucky she was not to have any spinal damage.

'Fuck me, I never even thought about being paralyzed. Thank God.'

Her terrified expression got a pat on her shoulder.

"You really are doing remarkably well considering. And the swelling around your face and neck is starting to subside, and your black eyes have already faded quite a bit." He gave her a thumbs up.

"I wanted to let you know that I've scheduled another MRI in the morning to make sure the bleeds are under control. And now that your swelling is going down, I'll be able to evaluate any other damage that might have been hidden before. I don't want you to worry. I don't foresee any issues, but when it comes to the brain, you can't be too careful. Now, do you have any questions for me?" His bedside manner was very good.

She liked him.

"Memory?" She still liked the one word asks since her throat was easily aggravated.

"That will take as much time as it takes. Sorry, there is no way to know. Each person is different. But my guess is that you'll never remember the car crash and maybe not even the day or days prior."

She nodded.

Again, that just sucks out loud.

He patted her shoulder again. "I'll tell Adam to bring you another popsicle, and tomorrow we're going to start you on light meals and move you off liquids only, that should help with the healing process, and it will also aid in getting some of your strength back. You're still going to get pain meds to help sleep. At least for the next week or so. I'll see you at the MRI."

She thanked him.

After her second popsicle they put more pain medication in her IV, and she slept a dreamless sleep. Just registering James' return for the nightshift before lights out. He shaved. 'Good.'

The morning scan showed that her brain was in fact back to its normal size, and the three hairline fractures were healing nicely. Better yet the two hematomas had shrunk down from silver dollar size to dime size. And there were no other anomalies and no other bleeds. Dr Jarvis was very pleased with her progress and gave the order to move her out of ICU and into her own room.

'Yes!' Again, it's the little things.

After a sponge bath, which is embarrassing but very much needed and a fresh gown, her two new nurses got Becca into bed and comfortable in a private room.

Well, as comfortable as one can be in a hospital bed with casts on both your arm and leg. And let's not even talk about the catheter.

Ick to the nth degree.

She was going to miss Hollie and would have to remember to send her flowers.

This would also be the first time she actually saw her face in the mirror.

'Fuck, I look like I just went ten rounds with Joe Frazier and forgot to put my hands up.'

Not an attractive look by any means.

She was also grateful that she didn't see herself before the swelling started to go down. Damn!

Her complexion was quite pale and for the first time in her life, she actually thought that she looked too thin.

Not a fan of scales as you may remember, her best guess is that she'd lost at least 15 pounds since the car accident

Dr Lawson had stopped by and told her that she'd be moved to the rehab ward in another four weeks or so. They wanted her to start physical therapy which is another progression to help get her strength back. And her mobility.

He confirmed her hunch regarding her weight. The bed in ICU had a built-in scale, and they tracked her weight loss, which is pretty normal for such severe injuries.

Getting back on solid foods would help with that, and she still needed time and nutrients for the ribs to finish healing. Plus, she also needed to recover from the surgery removing her spleen before they even considered any rehabilitation.

He went on and explained that she could live a normal life without her spleen but a simple infection could put her in the hospital. And others might actually kill her. For those reasons she would need to take antibiotics for the next several years. Maybe for the rest of her life.

Great news. And this all coming from the doctor she liked.

'Again, FUCK!'

Dr Jackass, aka Gering, stopped by as well to inform her that the casts on her arm would remain for at least four more weeks, minimum. Six to eight weeks for the leg as it now had a metal rod.

Again, that totally blows, and she was glad when he left.

Her whole body was still in a constant dull pain. But she could tell it was getting better... slowly. Oh, so fucking slowly.

'Maybe I should sue that jerk after all'.

She laughed at the thought, 'oh hell no', still a bad idea on so many levels with those damn ribs.

It wasn't until the following day, her twenty-fifth in hospital, that she finally convinced James to go home to Billings and take care of his construction business.

She also told her loving nephew and his sweet partner to get the asses back to work as well. And mentioned to Jake that he should ask Hollie on a date if she was single. And would he please take her flowers as a 'thank you'.

Oh yeah, huge eye roll from her much-loved nephew, but he told his thoughtful aunt that he would act as her delivery boy.

Still, he was the hardest to convince to leave. She told him to come see her in a week or so and that was enough to appease him, barely.

Yep, her favorite.

The police showed up two days later and asked if she remembered any part of the accident and she honestly didn't. Although she did tell them that she'd been trying.

Dr Lawson made the point of telling them, in front of Becca, that it would be better if they came back in another few weeks, but Lieutenant Garrison continued his inquiry refusing to take the doctor's advice.

He asked about the rental car and again, she couldn't even remember why she had a rental since she usually just drove her Enclave up from Ely.

Becca also told him that she was rarely up this time of the year so, that was also baffling to her. And perhaps they should ask her nephew if he might know what she was doing on the cabin road. She'd forgotten to ask him.

Yep.

Brain mush!

She was told that Jake had already been questioned and it was routine to ask everyone involved the same or similar questions.

No, he would not fill-in any blanks.

Moments later the officer dropped the bombshell that put Becca into the tailspin of her life.

"Mrs. Jackson, just one more question and this is regarding your passenger that was killed in the accident. How well did you know, Mary Louise Neilson?"

He showed her the photo of her dead best friend.

"WHAT!? NO! Mary's never come to the cabin with me." She just stared at the photo in utter disbelief. It looked like she was laying on an autopsy table.

The tears and shock gave them their answer and crushed her world.

'Mary had been killed in the wreck?

That can't be right.'

A fucking accident she can't remember, and she had no idea why Mary would have been with her and in a rental car to boot.

'Fucking hell - I Killed my best friend!'

Becca starting shaking uncontrollably as she starred at her best friend's corpse.

She just missed puking on the police officer that was standing next to her.

Dr Lawson ended their interview and had to sedate Becca when she started to hyperventilate with heart-crushing sobs.

She also managed to rebreak one of her almost healed ribs.

The hospital called in a grief counselor the next day but she wouldn't communicate with anyone.

She cried from the minute; she woke until they were forced to sedate her so her body would rest.

Dr Jarvis was concerned with her high blood pressure; Dr Lawson was concerned about everything, and Dr Gering never came by.

The stupid counselor they called prattled on about, time healing all wounds.

'Fucking moron'.

It was four days later when the uncontrollable sobs were replaced with a severe depression, and she no longer would eat or drink much of anything.

Not like she'd been doing much of that anyway.

Most things she tried to eat came right back up and that hurt her healing ribs and her throat so, she just gave up trying.

The tears were never too far away. And without must warning they would fall with no sign of stopping.

Both Dr Lawson and Dr Jarvis gave her the lecture that her body needed fuel to mend, and they didn't want to have to put in a feeding tube but would if they had to.

She told them that she wanted to sign a DNR.

They couldn't refuse her after the psych department said, she was totally within her rights and of sound mind.

'Ha! Fuckers! Screw your feeding tube.' She hated everyone but mostly she hated herself.

After much cajoling, she finally agreed to try Ensure if they'd take the IV out. They reluctantly agreed with the stipulation that she had to make an effort to drink several a day.

She could swallow just fine and could take pain medication orally when needed. So, the IV wasn't necessary.

The biggest issue was her lack of appetite since her 'give a damn' was severely broken.

Still, she managed to drink just enough nutrients to keep them somewhat off her back.

Every night when the lights went out, she let the tears fall freely and knew her heart was broken.

Her thoughts would turn gloomy and black as she faced the darkness alone.

The nightmares were causing her to get very little sleep... she'd wake up screaming but no sound came out.

They weren't about the accident itself, just the images of her best friend... dead in the photo, she'd been shown.

'I killed my best friend. I should have died too? Why the fuck did I live?'

But somewhere in her heart and in her wacked out brain, she knew there was a reason to live. She just didn't know what.

That caused a different pain and more sleepless nights.

The emotional pain of losing Mary was worse than anything the accident inflicted on her physically.

It was almost a week since the horrific news about her best friend when Dr Lawson apparently called Jake and asked him to please come. He hated to bother him, but he was very concerned about his aunt's mental status along with her physical wellbeing since she wasn't healing as quickly as she should be and had lost another ten pounds.

Along with her grief... Becca was dealing with the lack of memory about her life the past few months and it wasn't just the accident that was making her heart hurt. She felt another loss of something or someone. Her heart seemed to be in constant earth-crushing pain.

'What was Jake saying a couple weeks ago... she knew she needed to ask him something? But what?' Even her thoughts were pissing her off now.

It was a bit of a break from the sadness that was ever present to try and remember the past several months.

With each passing day she was feeling a bit better, and her ribs were letting her breath much easier, still she didn't care.

When Jake arrived, she was crying, which wasn't unusual these past several days but the look of desolation on her face brought on his own tears.

"Oh shit... Aunt Bec's. I'm so sorry. I should have told you about Mary, but the doctors wanted you to concentrate on healing. They had no idea what her death would cause, but I did, so I didn't tell you. Pops and I had a fight about it. Justin wanted to tell you too. We couldn't save her Becca. She died on impact. I don't believe she suffered."

More talking to the air than her nephew. "No, suffering is reserved for the living."

He was wiping his eyes and hers, but her tears wouldn't be contained.

Her loving nephew just sat and held her hand and let her tears fall.

They sedated her again that night in the hopes of her getting some much-needed rest.

Jake never left her side.

When she woke and saw him sitting there, still holding her hand, looking so concerned and appearing as if he'd been crying all night. She could see her anguish reflected in his eyes.

At that moment she realized that her dying would have broken his heart and she wouldn't want him to suffer like that.

But she felt so lost.

"I killed my best friend, Jakey. I don't know how I can live with this pain?" She sobbed but brought it under control for the first time in a week. Vowing to herself to not make her nephew feel worse than he already did for not telling her.

"No Becca you didn't. The guy who sideswiped you did. You need to remember that this was not your fault. It was just a very horrible and tragic accident." He had tears back in his eyes.

She nodded.

She attempted a smile for the first time, in what seemed like forever, to let her very sweet and caring nephew know how much she appreciated him, but it didn't reach her eyes.

The head can grasp things much quicker than the heart.

Justin's sudden entrance startled them both. He handed Jake a large coffee and Becca a smoothie. His look told her not fuck with him.

It reminded her of someone.

She asked them both to just talk about what they'd been doing since the last time she saw them, as she tried to drink the delicious fruity beverage.

Their banter made her feel some normalcy which had been lacking. She loved the JJ's and cherished them both for coming to rescue her, again.

After careful hugs and kisses, they said their good-byes, and she thanked them for coming.

Jake asked to stay for a few more days but his stubborn aunt told him no.

If you're wondering, she managed about one third of the smoothie. Grief is a process.

The thought of never talking with or seeing Mary again still brought on a monumental sadness but she didn't cry every time, which was progress. Still her heart always hurt.

On day eleven or twelve in her private room, she realized, she was getting quite a nice selection of floral arrangements.

She felt quite loved by her family, who were going way overboard and keeping 'Flowers.com' quite busy.

She asked one of the nurses, if anyone near her was without any.

She was told that two older ladies didn't have flowers and then asked, if she could share hers, minus the cards of course.

She'd only stayed in the hospital once before when she had to get her appendix out, and she remembered that the woman in the bed next to hers didn't get any flowers, and one day, she asked her mom to please give her one of the arrangements she'd received. She liked making her roommate smile.

She didn't need any kind of thank you...' being human is the best part of humanity. Her grandfather taught her that... he was the only person, she felt that loved her unconditionally when she was younger.

His ashes were in the meadow above the cabin. He was one of her favorite people that used to roam the earth.

'He'd take care of Mary in heaven.' That thought made her happy and sad.

"Anonymous please and thank you for doing this." She smiled at the accommodating nurse.

She had lost track of the names of some of the nurses, there were over twenty on her floor but the delivery nurse was Robyn.

One of her favorites.

She was round, pretty and had a great laugh. And an endless supply of popsicles.

Still the one thing they could get her to eat, on occasion.

Robyn returned to tell Becca that both ladies wanted to thank the thoughtful person who brightened their day.

She nodded.

There are a lot of hours in the day to just think. Maybe too much time.

This day Becca was thinking how strange it seemed that she could recall her childhood, the horrid experience that others called high school, she even could recall her college days but still nothing for the past several months.

'It's just fucking weird.'

She always smiled, whenever she thought or said the 'f' word. But still no clue why she wasn't supposed to use it, again odd.

Becca woke the next morning, again not knowing exactly what day of the week it was, she was getting use to that but this day she felt really depressed.

And it wasn't her injuries, or the loss of her best friend, although that was an ever-present ache... this day she felt like she'd lost something in her life that was so very important.

She'd had this thought quite often over the past month, but this day it was stronger. And whatever it was exactly, just might be lost forever.

She so wished she could remember. Her heart felt like it was breaking for a whole new reason.

It was sometimes hard being alone, but she didn't want to be a nuisance to her family either and they needed to get back to their own lives.

Still, she felt a sadness this day. She was now on day thirty-nine in the hospital. Summer had ended and autumn was crisply in the air.

"Hey Aunt Becs." Jake was grinning.

His surprise visit brightened her mood immediately.

"Hey Jakey, what are you doing here? Not that I'm not thrilled to see you." She smiled at her very sweet nephew with the love she'd always had for him.

"You're looking so much better. How are you, really?" He knew she was still dealing with her grief.

"Better. I promise." He sat and took her hand after kissing her cheek.

"It's nice to see the swelling is gone. I can see my beautiful aunt coming back to me. Just a bit paler and a lot thinner. You're still not eating. Becs, I'm worried about you. I still have another week of family leave time, please let me stay."

She shook her head.

It was one of the hardest things she'd done, since part of her would really like to wake up with him there.

"Fine. But you have to promise me that you'll eat. It looks like you've dropped another five pounds since last time I was here. And that was just six days ago." He didn't look happy.

She nodded and told him she'd try.

"Okay. Well one of the reasons I'm here is to bring you some items I managed to locate. I didn't find your phone so I bought you a new one on my plan since I wasn't sure who your provider was. You now have an Idaho number but once you get home you can get it changed back. The bigger issue is that all your contacts are lost unless you saved them to the 'cloud'." He handed her the phone.

"Thanks Jake".

"Well, now at least you can get a hold of me and in turn I can call to check on you. Without going through the hospital switchboard. So, can Pops, J and even Mark." He wrinkles his nose on his brother's name.

She couldn't help but chuckle.

Still her favorite.

"I also programmed my phone number, Justin's, Pops and even that jerk brother of mine married to the skank." He smirked.

Oh yeah, she so loved the little shit. A button pusher in his own right.

She hadn't seen Mark, Jake's older brother, for almost two years but his was one of the biggest arrangements in her room. In fact, a fresh one arrived each week. Maybe he was feeling a bit guilty since he'd not come to visit.

According to Jake, Mark did spend several nights with her while, she was in the coma but couldn't handle her almost dying. His guilt over the huge fight two years ago was the reason, as stated earlier.

But like us all, sometimes our Becca can be a cynic.

She'd never be able to disprove that he was there so, she decided to take it at face value and would thank him, if and when she ever saw him again.

"Thank you so much Jake, it's very thoughtful of you."

She was looking at the items he brought. 'Wallet, iPod, jewelry bag and IPad with a huge, cracked screen that would never be used again.

She'd miss her library but knew she could retrieve all her favorites when she bought a new one. It was more than she thought she'd ever see again.

But it made her think of Mary and her heart gave her a 'twinge.'

Her ever-observant cop nephew gave her hand a squeeze.

"I also got you new headphones and charger for your iPod since those were also lost." He had his dad's smile.

"Give us a hug sweet boy". And he did. It helped across the board.

They had a nice visit before he had to head home. Bittersweet to be sure.

He finally cleared up one major question she'd been wondering about. 'Why was she even on the cabin road that late in the summer?'.

He told her about throwing his pops a surprise 60th birthday bash, and how he'd called and convinced her to come and forgive James in the process. He was a great son, and she so loved him.

He was also feeling guilty because if he hadn't asked her to come, she wouldn't have been in that ghastly accident and wouldn't have lost her best friend.

She told him it wasn't his fault either and reminded him that the guy who sideswiped her was still the one to blame.

He'd pointed that out to her just a few days prior.

He nodded.

She finally asked if he knew what she'd been doing the past few months, and he told he wasn't allowed to tell her anything. The doctors wanted her memories to be hers and hers alone.

Made sense, in a 'sucky' kind of way.

She could tell that he had one piece of information that was driving him crazy but he still held his tongue.

Stubborn men in her family.

Before Jake left, he plugged in her iPod and told her he'd be happy to buy her a new IPad if she wished. She declined.

He made sure her phone was within her reach. And with a kiss on the cheek and 'love you', she watched him head out the door.

He also let her know that Hollie was indeed married but like always, she had good taste in woman. He shrugged and grinned as he left.

Hollie had come down and visited Becca a few days prior to thank her for the flowers so, she already knew that but smiled as Jake left.

A dinner tray was brought in a bit later, ever hopeful that they could get her to eat but nothing looked edible, hospital food. Yuck!

Of course, still not having much of an appetite didn't help their cause. But she had promised her nephew that she would try.

So, she put the Jell-O off to the side for later.

The stubborn streak isn't just on the male side of the family.

But then again, who doesn't like Jell-O.

Becca opted for a nap in the hopes, she'd wake not feeling quite so forlorn.

'Maybe I should have let Jake stay'.

Woulda. Coulda. Shoulda.

She dreamt without nightmares for the first time since the police told her about the death of her friend.

Flashes mostly of blue skis, lifejackets, bears, eagles and jet skis.

What a weird ass dream, not remembering anything particular, just bits and pieces.

She hated jet skis, noisy little fuckers, never needed a lifejacket on her lake but did love blue skis.

And the bears and eagles were ever present in Northern Idaho but not something she usually dreamt about.

It was full on night when she woke. The tray was gone, and her room was fairly dark for a change.

The figure in the doorway blocking even more light, scared the living crap out of her.

He moved suddenly to her side and kissed her lips.

She should have been terrified or at least offended but she knew that kiss.

She stared at the beautiful face behind those lips without knowing exactly who he was.

Bald head, beard and absolutely stunning, even in the dim light, she could see how handsome he was.

She sensed a familiar pull to him.

"Oh my God Becca, I've been trying to find you for weeks. When you didn't call me and then didn't check into your flight home, I just didn't know what to think. Do you know how crazy worried I've been? I've called your phone at least five hundred times, texted you and emailed you about ten times a day. I got stuck in Texas much longer than expected and with the New York situation it took me longer than expected to get my ass up here to look for you."

He took a breath.

"I couldn't remember your nephew's name so when I called the sheriff's department I must have sounded like a lunatic. I finally went to your Ely house and then drove to the cabin, but no one was there. I finally had the good sense to go to the sheriff's department in person to find your nephew, whose name was still eluding me but after giving them your name, I got to his partner. And he remembered me from several months ago when I went in for permits. He wouldn't tell me anything except that you were in a horrific accident, but after some major pleading he told me what hospital you were in but only after he called your nephew, Jake, for his permission." He had tears in his eyes.

He was rambling, and she had no idea what exactly he was talking about regarding New York and Texas, but she knew his voice.

And she wanted him to keep talking to her.

His next kiss was more intimate, and again she felt drawn to him. And she liked his kisses, a lot.

He was sitting on the bed and holding her hand while stoking her knuckles with his thumb.

Finally, her eyes adjusted to the ambient light, and she found herself staring into the most beautiful green eyes and she smiled.

"Hi Cain."

And the floodgates opened, and she started to cry. She was so ecstatic to see the love of her life but felt the loss of Mary in the most powerful way.

The tears in his eyes started to fall down his cheeks again and that caught her off guard.

They actually helped calm her own.

Her heart was having issues of which way to feel. Utter joy or deep despair.

Survivors Guilt! True survivors' guilt.

Not like when her husband died. She was more relieved which brought on a different kind of guilt. What kind of person is glad when someone dies? She always knew that's why she avoided daylight hours since she was afraid people would see that she wasn't a grieving widow. How bad of a person did that make her? That question would be for another day. Or maybe she should just let it go.

Because, sitting right beside her was the piece of the puzzle that had been missing from her aching heart. The real reason her life was still worth living. Her soulmate.

"Mary's dead and I've been missing you so much. I can't remember anything that's happened in the past few months. It's like a big dark hole but I feel completely drawn to you. It's just..." His kiss stopped her talking and he wrapped her in his arms the best he could. Minding the cast on the left arm.

Once he released her lips, he wiped away her tears and his.

"Oh baby, I'm so sorry, but would you please tell me everything you've been told about your injuries and the accident."

He kissed her hand and moved from her bed where he'd perched and took the chair Jake had sat in just a few hours prior. He dabbed her eyes and his again, as she proceeded to explain what all the doctors had told her about her injuries, and what she'd been told from the JJs about the catastrophic wreck that took her best friend's life.

He cringed when she told him about how they had to use the 'jaws of life' to extract her from the wreckage causing the second break in her left leg.

After asking permission he lifted the sheet to look at her injuries, most of the cuts and abrasions had healed thank goodness and his fingers trailed from her right ankle up her right leg, to her once bruised and broken ribs, her scar where her spleen used to be, up her neck and down her right arm to the hand he reclaimed and kissed again. She watched him and never felt embarrassed... he radiated unconditional love.

'I know his touch... I've been longing for him.' was her only actual thought. Tears still flowed down her cheek.

She told him what all three doctors had told her about the plan of moving her in another week or so, to recovery in the hopes to start physical therapy on her arm. Her leg would be a couple of weeks after.

He wiped her tears again and gave her another tender kiss as he sat back on the bed to be closer.

"Baby, would it be okay if I hired a physical therapist and a nurse and you came home with me instead? I can't bear to have you here any longer than necessary. You belong with me." His eyes showed the deep love he had for her.

She nodded. She didn't want him to leave, ever. It was the first time in well over a month that she felt whole, and she told him exactly that.

"Becca sweetheart, I'm not going anywhere without you. You are the love of my existence. And again, I'm so sorry about Mary." He kissed her forehead and worked his way down to her lips.

His kisses made her so very content, but she did wonder where his home was exactly, but then realized it would be wherever he was. She did in fact love him. For that she was sure of, her heart told her so.

"You're so thin Becca, too thin. You've lost at least thirty pounds. I know you're not eating. Joel's going to fix that right quick." And he smiled.

She liked that smile a great deal. It was her smile.

Reaching up and caressing his cheek, Cain kissed the palm of her hand.

"You know, you look really tired, and I think you've lost weight too. And out of curiosity, who's Joel?"

He laughed. It was one of the best sounds she'd ever heard.

"All in good time my girl. Your memories will come back. And don't you dare worry about me, I'll be fine now that I've found you." He was looking at her broken IPad that was still on the tray. When he turned back, he had the most loving smile. She felt an utter peace come over her.

As he spoke and her mind calmed itself, one powerful memory came into focus. "Would you please hand me that little velvet bag."

He did.

She opened it and found her mom's diamond earrings, a pair of gold hoops Mary had given her for her 50th birthday, which gave her a happy memory of her friend, and then she found what she was seeking... a very precious silver ring with a raven and eagle etched into the metal.

'Alaskan Lovebirds.'

She was beaming. 'He gave it to her in Juneau. Now she just needed to remember why the fuck were they in Alaska? Maybe he lived there. Huh?'

Baby steps.

He took the ring from her and placed it on her right hand. Then kissed it.

"It's supposed to be on the other hand, but we'll wait until your cast is off." He kept her hand encased with his.

"I may not remember all the details right now, but I do know that I love you Cain with my entire heart and soul. Thank you for finding me." Tears returned, very happy tears this time.

"Always and forever Becca." He gave her another tender kiss and looked into eyes. "I will never let you out of my sight again. And now more than ever I want you to please marry me?"

She smiled and asked if he'd mind waiting and repeating that request when she didn't look like the 'bride of Frankenstein' and could remember a few more details.

"You are the most beautiful thing I've seen in over a month but yes baby. I can do that." He gave her another kiss and her world began to right itself.

EPILOG

"I hate your fucking guts!" She winced.

"Don't care... ten more reps. You aren't going to walk with a limp on my watch."

She did as she was told but it hurt like hell, and she was thinking about all kinds of revenge.

'Physical Therapists are the spawn of Satan'.

Hers was named Jon Smith.

Yep, no shit.

He was five foot four inches and built like a brick shithouse. His entire body was muscle and when he really pissed her off, she asked him if the other members of the 'Lollipop Guild' missed him... trust me, he deserved that and more.

Cain spent the first several days with her, while she went through physical therapy on her newly uncast arm. Jon wasn't easy on her at all, and Cain had a very hard time watching her wince and at one-point cry.

Jon actually banned him from coming, if he interfered again with one of their sessions. 'Little prick'.

Nope, Mr Smith wasn't afraid of anyone. And even though Cain was paying him… the very strict therapist set the ground rules.

Still the first time, she asked him that somewhat offensive question Cain lost it and had to leave their stateroom.

Yes, as a matter of fact, he did choke on the water he was drinking. Very good.

She still had impeccable timing with her comments.

Becca finished with the weights on her now very sore leg, and he told her to walk for ten minutes on the treadmill and then call it a day.

She was ever so happy when she was healthy enough to move her work outs from their stateroom to the gym.

It really did suck that she couldn't move very well around the yacht for the first several weeks on board. He had suggested that they go to the Nevada house to begin with, but she was totally against ever going there again.

It brought back too many memories of Mary.

Cain gave in, and they went back to their home on the water.

He would help her to the living room on occasion, but her happiest day was when she was strong enough to use crutches and finally get rid of that fucking catheter.

Tomorrow would be her arm therapy again and some much-needed stretching. Those were easier days since he'd been working on her arm for over five weeks. It was almost back to normal in strength, but flexibility was still a small issue. The leg was just finishing week one and painful didn't even begin to cover it.

They would be starting water therapy in another week or so, and that made Becca very happy.

Cain made arrangements with the Marina to let her use their pool for an hour each morning before it opened to the rest of the guests.

Yes, he did stipulate that he would be there for all water activities. Still a bit anxious when it came to that.

Hey, better than anal or control freak. Both still fit.

Becca did have a limp but even after the first week, she could tell all the therapy was helping, little by little. She wasn't about to tell 'the spawn' that.

Her left leg looked anorexic compared to the right, but 'Satin' promised her it would even out after week four or five, just like her arm.

She felt rode hard and put up wet when she made it down to the main salon of the yacht. That made her laugh since it was just a few months back she thought the same thing in an entirely different scenario.

Joel handed her a protein shake and gave her a wink and a grin, as she limped by with just one crutch now. An improvement to be sure.

She thanked him and started drinking it on her way to the stateroom.

The first couple weeks back on the yacht were awkward to be sure. And every time Joel saw her, he cringed and tried to get her to eat or drink something. With his and Cain's constant badgering, okay, so it was more love and concern but, in her mind, it was more like nagging. When she finally began to eat, her health started to improve. Just like all her doctors told her. They'd managed to put twenty pounds back onto her, but she was still down fifteen.

Again... Baby steps.

Cain had called both Frank and Joel after he finally found Becca and told them of her vast number of injuries, they each volunteered to come back and help with her care.

So, very sweet.

Frank was designing some of the upgrades that he and Cain wanted to have done to the engines before their next voyage. This wouldn't happen for another six to eight months. And Joel returned as everyone's nutritionist and chef.

He also spent time just keeping Becca company when the chance arose. Usually when Cain was working.

Always welcome. He was after all, one of her favorite people.

Joel's finance Steve would fly down every few weeks for a weekend visit.

Becca was thrilled that their relationship was moving forward.

About damn time too.

Yes, that did make her think of her own. Thanks for keeping up.

Stella even came back every other week for a few days and did a mass clean. She's still a powerhouse.

Becca loved them all for helping care for her. She'd never be able to thank them enough for their wonderful support.

Before she returned to the yacht, Cain had to convince her doctors, brother and nephew that it was the best thing. The doctors and James were easy in comparison but in the end, Jake came around and could see the love they had for each other and agreed but only after Becca and Cain swore to call him with a weekly update.

She really loved the little shit.

Of course, what really helped and made the biggest difference in her recovery was when her memory returned.

It was weird though... she had been back on board 'SIRA' for almost two and a half weeks when one morning she woke up and everything was there.

How Cain and she met, when he came by the cabin the first time for coffee, when he hit her in the head with a lifejacket, the amazing trip to Alaska, their copious amounts of sex... Oh Damn!

She also remembered everyone on the yacht, the trip to San Diego, their drive to Nevada and even the details of why she and Mary were going north together... all her memories had returned except for the flight to

Spokane, the actual drive to the cabin and the accident itself.

Again, small favors.

She really hoped she'd never remember the details that ended up killing her best friend.

Cain filled in the blanks regarding his trip to New York since her accident took place first.

She did remember him having to go and why but no details of the trip.

Well, the whole thing ended up being a huge surprise to him as well. They offered him a promotion. They never had any desire to lose him but wanted to make the offer in person and thank him for his twenty-plus years of service.

The complaint he'd received earlier was filed and forgotten. He was never meeting with HR, that was a total scam from one of the managing partners, Wayne Hughes, to keep Cain guessing.

He'd known and worked with him for over fifteen years.

The only issue with this new title; 'Western Division Director', meant that Cain would have to have a permanent office where he'd oversee four to six financial advisors, a notary, two office staff and a receptionist. To make the offer sweeter, they did agree to make San Diego their new western branch location.

The new position had a number of perks as well, including a very handsome raise and six weeks of vacation each year. The retirement package was also exceedingly substantial.

He called Wayne to let him know about Becca and her accident. So, now, knowing the situation with his love, they gave him until the first of March to make his decision.

In the meantime, he was still wanting to go to the Hawaiian Islands for at least five to six weeks over January and February. It would be a working vacation, but he'd still have more than enough free time to enjoy the trip.

His real hope was to leave mid-December but that would depend on Becca's rehab.

At this rate it was more than likely they would ring in the New Year in the fiftieth state, maybe.

She had always thought he was planning on taking his yacht but he told her that 'SIRA' wasn't equipped for the twenty-three-hundred-mile journey so they would fly over and rent a house on the beach for their winter excursion.

The Texas situation was greatly improved as well.

His father had a heart attack the day they arrived in Ely and his mother called the following day and asked him to please come home since his dad had to have a triple bypass.

His recovery was a bit slower than they'd hoped and he ended up having to stay in the hospital for an extra two and a half weeks with a serious infection. That postponed Cain's trip to New York and in turn, delayed him finding Becca sooner. He also had to make one more trip back to San Antonia after his trip east to make sure that his dad was on the mend.

He still felt guilty for not coming north sooner but Becca was just happy he came. He completed her. And told him that every time he brought it up.

She also reminded him that he couldn't do anything for her, since her mind and body had to do some major healing of their own.

Robert was home with Mabel now and doing so much better. Cain and his mother found some common ground to make their peace, his dad.

Their relationship would never be perfect, but they seemed to be more at ease with each other.

He calls them both every week and a half to check-in. And there was even talk of he, and Becca going to San Antonio for Thanksgiving, but they opted for the following year.

Give everyone in his life a chance to recover fully.

Jake gets called every week as promised and given a detailed explanation of his aunt's recovery, usually, Cain makes the call and then hands the phone over to Becca for a friendly chat. As mentioned before, her nephew is a tad anal, but he comes by it honestly.

Yep, still her favorite. Always will be.

Becca calls James every few weeks to keep him in the loop regarding her progress. But when she doesn't, he's quick to call her.

Again, anal but very sweet.

He also informed her that he would buy her half of the cabin if, and when she ever wanted to sell it but let her know that she was required to spend a month there each and every summer. Both she and Cain. He wanted to keep the property in the family and didn't want it to be an issue between his two sons. Smart dad.

It made her ever so happy to have her brother back in her life.

A life that she can't ever take for granted.

Hell, even Mark managed to call once in a while and give her an update on the kids.

Ashley and Collin were looking forward to coming to stay at the cabin with their great Aunt Becs and her man Cain (Ashley's term) for a few days the following summer. No parents allowed.

Little Gail, who doesn't remember Becca very well, is coming out with her dad for a day when he comes to pick up the other two.

And, 'No' Amy will not be coming.

Apparently, a very precocious Ashley asked if she could have a divorce for her birthday.

She felt her life would be greatly improved if she could go live with her grandpa or her Uncle Jake. They would make sure she got to see her Aunt Becca whom she loved very much. And missed a lot.

That request broke Mark's heart but also made him realize that his little girl was very unhappy and changes were necessary.

He vowed to mend his and Becca's relationship which in turn he hoped would fix his and his oldest daughter's.

Hard to tell with teenage hormones playing a factor. But what the hell, worth a try.

According to Jake, he also put his foot down with Amy and her constant bullshit with regards to members of his family, and she backed down.

First smart thing that woman ever did besides marrying Mark.

To be a fly on the wall for that conversation.

Ashley turned thirteen a few weeks back and got her first iPhone so, she was keeping her Aunt Becca entertained with all sorts of text messages and memes throughout the day. She loved having her great-niece back in her life. Collin is more like his dad and less into texting or even chatting on the phone, so Ashley gives updates on both her siblings.

Cain got Becca's cell phone moved onto his plan and switched the Idaho number back to her Nevada number since everyone knew that one.

Her life was so much better now that her mind and body were healing… still… she fought bouts of depression regarding the loss of Mary from time to time.

When she actually stopped to think about going back to the cabin, she was both happy and terrified.

She had a very bad week when Liam called and told her that he'd found Mary's will, and that she had left everything to Becca.

'Fuck! Really.'

She didn't have a clue that Mary had done that, and it threw her for a loop since it made her remember, it was because of her that her friend died.

Yes, she was quite aware that it was just an accident but guilt and grief, as stated before, are a process.

That and the head and heart aren't always on the same page. Also mentioned before.

Liam asked to buy the cottage, and she sold it to him for one dollar after discussing the idea with Cain.

With the settlement money Mary received, Becca paid off the mortgage.

It was the least she could do. Liam was going through his own grief at the time.

He didn't blame Becca and that helped... some.

Her very caring man stayed close that week and made sure his arms were there whenever she needed them.

He would often hold her tight when her grief would take hold and consume her. A fissure in her heart was a result of that epic loss, one that didn't exactly heal but after that horrid week, she was having fewer days of utter sadness.

She missed her friend.

She always would.

Cain offered on several occasions to go with her to therapy, if she thought it would help. She said the best therapy was having his arms around her.

Again, and again... Grief is a process... Baby Steps.

Huh...

Time does heal all wounds. 'Fucking moron was right'.

Becca finally settled her claim with the insurance company of the guy who caused the accident and that covered her stay in the hospital, the private nurse she had to have for the first couple weeks on the yacht and the demonic physical therapist. Cain started-off paying him but after a few weeks he was reimbursed.

It also put a tidy sum in the bank.

Becca insisted that Cain be put on the account to manage her finances.

He actually agreed to a compromise.

When she talked about selling the Ely house, Cain convinced her to wait for one year before making any rash decisions.

In the meantime, he got a caretaker for the property and had all the mail forwarded to San Diego.

He also found his present she'd left on the island in the kitchen when he went and packed up their belongings.

Including her new dresses.

It was the one and only time he left her and that wouldn't have happened, if Joel, Frank and the nurse weren't on the yacht to look after her.

Plus; at that point, she was still bed ridden with round the clock care.

Mentioned the catheter... Ick!

He made sure she was okay with his being gone for a couple days and bought her a new IPad so, when he did video chat with her, she could see him better.

She was also thrilled to get her library back. Lots of hours with nothing to do when you're stuck in bed.

Cain was quite happy; he was alone when he unwrapped her special gift since the beautiful and thoughtful photo/scrapbook album brought tears to his eyes.

He came close to losing her again, and that can never happen.

He framed the precious card with the note she wrote him, just over two months prior and put that on his desk. The album was given a place of honor on the bookshelf in his study.

He felt her love each time he looked at these prized possessions.

The memory that overwhelmed Becca the most these past two weeks, was Cain being her favorite sex toy. She missed his prowess... A Lot!

Plus, he was way behind on the twelve hundred.

He put his foot down and told her, he was off limits until all casts were removed and her arm and leg were on the mend.

She wasn't even allowed to use her newest skill.

Yep, fully recovered memory.

Party Pooper!

She mentioned only once about his arbitrary number of orgasms.

"Don't fret about that baby, I'll catch up. Believe me." His wink and that statement caused a very warm feeling throughout Becca's whole body.

'Damn him!'

Of course, he still held her every night and she woke in his arms each morning.

She even started to read to him again.

They were giving Mark Twain a go.

Intimate and lovely.

It was truly, her version of heaven on earth!

When she entered their stateroom, Cain was waiting for her. He took the almost empty glass that held a very wonderful protein drink and put it on his nightstand, he then took her hand and led her into the bathroom, helped her out of her very sweaty workout clothes and into the waiting jetted tub.

He joined her.

It was her favorite part of physical therapy.

The hot water felt so good and relaxed her aching muscles.

"How was it today my girl?"

"Fucking brutal… that man is truly the spawn of Satan." But she laughed and so did Cain.

If you're curious… the word 'fuck' was no longer an issue. Almost losing her made him realize that.

Pretty fucking quick actually.

She did remember that he was the one that didn't like her saying the word… too fucking bad.

Button Pusher that she is.

She leaned back against his shoulder and closed her eyes.

"Do you know how much I love you Cain?"

His hands moved up her sides, and he started to caress her breasts.

"No more than I love you baby, always and forever."

'Well, this is new.'

Her eyes flew open.

Usually, it was a shoulder and back massage only.

'Yes! Yes! Yes!'

Her breasts came to life at his touch, as did her libido.

When his lips and tongue started attacking her earlobe she turned and captured his mouth with hers. Oh, she'd missed him.

Dry spell over and then some.

Hot Damn!

"Becca sweetheart, I've been waiting a very long time for this day." She nodded in agreement since she was still catching her breath.

Talk about a workout.

He had her cradled in his arms.

"How about spending the rest of the day in bed with me? As you pointed out, I'm behind on the twelve hundred. Or maybe we should just start over." Such a sexy and determined look.

"Yes please!" She didn't care how he interpreted that statement.

After weeks and weeks and weeks in bed recuperating from the accident, she didn't like just lying about anymore but, on this day, in his arms, she was quite happy to make an acceptation.

Happy and thoroughly loved.

Damn that man and his stamina.

Becca had just woken from a very nice nap and Cain was looking down at her and caressing her face.

"Baby, you mentioned you wanted me to wait and ask you the question I asked while you were still in the hospital, and it's been well over a month and a half now. Plus, your memories are all back and you can recall the first proposal... and you no longer look like the 'bride of Frankenstein', not that you ever did... so, how about it, you ready to marry me?"

His look was optimistic as he kissed the 'Alaskan Lovebird' ring that was now back on her left hand.

"So, sex is back on the table, but romance died. How very sad. Was it ill?" She just smirked at him.

He turned her over and smacked her ass pretty hard before pinning her on the bed and reclaiming her lips.

"Becca, I love you with every fiber of my being and I want to spend the rest of my life making love to you as my wife so stop all your stalling and tell me yes, or no?"

A SUNNY TUESDAY

Becca was enjoying a quiet morning with her coffee looking out over the lake that gave her such solace.

A lone eagle was out looking for some breakfast, and the sun was just starting to warm the day.

She was remembering the poem; she wrote so many moons ago about her love of the land and lake and the peace they had always brought her.

PEACE
Peace is not something you work for
Not something you strive to achieve
Peace is something deep inside
that certain things set free
Love is just a feeling that no one ever sees
It works together with the inner peace and
somehow comes to be
I've never understood the two or found
a special key
I only know the certain things that bring them
out in me
The beauty of Lake Pend Oreille on a clear starlite
night, holds so many memories dear

The strength of the mountains that surround the
lake, the darkness I used to fear
The so many times I used to dream
As I watched the stars above
And the long long walks I took through the trees
I used to always love
I find the things that bring me peace
And the things I truly love
Have always been the things
That I've been the most afraid of
The deep dark water of the lake
The secrets it's sure to hide
The calmness of the woods around
The fears were never justified
Around the mountains and by the lake
Brings my special peace to be
And however, far that I may go
No matter where that be
All my memories of the Land and Lake
Will keep alive the love in me.

This morning's peace was not to be since it was being interrupted by some idiot making a racket on a jet ski way too early for her liking.

So many of the neighboring cabins had them but they usually didn't break the tranquillity of their surroundings quite this early in the day.

As the annoying contraption went zipping by, she smiled at the very handsome man at the helm.

He waved and turned to head towards her.

She just shook her head.

As he pulled up to the dock his smile took her breath away. 'Damn, he's gorgeous.'

"Good morning, Beautiful. Glad to see that you're finally up and about this morning. Why don't you grab your lifejacket and come join me for a ride? " His green eyes were alit with the love he had for her.

"Well thank you my love, you're looking very handsome as well. I'm a bit tired since you wore my ass out last night, but a ride might be exactly what I need." She winked.

Damn, she loved him. More each and every day. If that's even possible.

"Baby, you just wait until tonight." What a wicked grin.

'Fuck me', that man and his stamina. She blushed.

He held out his hand and smiled as she climbed on the back of the jet ski. He loved that he could still cause that lovely shade of pink on her skin.

Yes, she had on a lifejacket.

REALLY!

I'm about to take you over my knee

"Thank you so much for bringing me back here and making me realize that I have far more good memories than bad. I love you with all my heart Mr. Curtis. And I've been meaning to tell you how fond I am of your new look." She gave him a tender kiss and stroked his fully grown out beard.

Well-trimmed of course.

"Why thank you, Mrs. Curtis. And I love you, always and forever."

He hit the throttle and off they went like a 'bat out of hell' across their lake.

Happily, Ever After is for fairy tales.

But wouldn't you settle for just being loved, unconditionally.

Thought so.

Me too!

But alas... 'That's All in my Daydream'.